PRAISE FOR CALIA WILDE

Wilde splices the action with heated scenes that
breathe intimacy and urgency

— BOOKLIFE

The way in which Wilde displayed sexual passion
upon the page was a fair mix of realism and
metaphor, which is what I like…I think *the payoff* can
be more explosive or have a greater impact if much
of what happens on the page can be experienced
through the reader's imagination. Wilde hit the nail
on the head.

— LIVE FREE LIVE RICH

VALENTINE'S CODE

CALIA WILDE

MISFIT INK BOOKS
MARYLAND, U.S.A.

Copyright ©2025 by A.R. Case writing as Calia Wilde

All rights reserved. No part of this publication may be reproduced, distributed, or transmitted in any form or by any means, including photocopying, recording, or other electronic or mechanical methods, without the prior written permission of the publisher, except in the case of brief quotations embodied in critical reviews and certain other noncommercial uses permitted by copyright law. For permission requests, write to the author, addressed "Attention: Permissions" at theAuthor@CaliaWilde.com.

Misfit Ink

5257 Buckeystown Pike, #215

Frederick, MD 21704

MisfitInkBooks.com

Ordering Information:

For details, contact theAuthor@CaliaWilde.com.

Disclaimer:

This book is a work of fiction. Any references to historical events, real people, or real locales are used fictitiously. Other names, characters, places, and incidents are the product of the author's imagination, and any resemblance to actual events or locales or persons, living or dead, is entirely coincidental.

Language, translation, and use: Not all phrases are translated. As the lead characters use/learn the varying languages, some notation of translation will occur (as the character understands it) is made. Whenever same-language speakers are the only characters on page, language use is inferred and not italicized. Translations may not be accurate for regional dialects due to author error. Certain phrases are taken from colloquial sayings and do not translate one-to-one to English - which this book is primarily written in.

The following is an indication and acknowledgement of potential content that may be upsetting or triggering, but is clearly not exhaustive:

Vulgar language, excessive or gratuitous violence, kidnapping (forceful deprivation of/disregard for personal autonomy), death or dying, and blood.

Valentine's Code is a work of fiction that may contain emotionally disturbing content. Please be aware of your own tolerance for the triggering content mentioned as well as use your best judgement about reading when your own emotional reserves are low. Sometimes it is the little things that can tip the balance into dark spaces.

Cover design, interior artwork, and layout: created by CT Cover Creations and Misfit Ink Books (MisfitInkBooks.com)

Front cover photography and interior art: Photography, background, interior art, and font treatments used under license through Adobe Stock. Any other fonts purchased under license or are supplied under open license for publishing use.

AI Disclaimer and Restriction: The author expressly prohibits any entity from using this publication for purposes of training artificial intelligence (AI) technologies to generate text, including without limitation technologies that are capable of generating works in the same style or genre as this publication. The author reserves all rights to license uses of this work for generative AI training and development of machine learning language models.

Generative AI was not used in the creation of this written work or the published content. Non-generative AI may be indicated as AI use in the metadata due to software-induced processing or false positives in detection software. Misfit Ink Books and the author believe in the power of human imagination and creativity, and supports creators who pursue their unique vision through dedication to craft and hard work.

INTRODUCTION

Notes on languages and translations, and deviations from the Chicago Manual of Style:

1. Google translate is *not* perfect. While the author did use it as a resource to double-check the meaning of certain words; phrasing and dialects required more in-depth research to represent a more accurate snapshot of how the exchanges would be spoken. Mistakes are my own.

2. Chicago Manual of Style: "generally advises italics for foreign words not in standard English dictionaries to signal them to the reader, but for fiction, especially by multilingual authors, it allows flexibility, suggesting regular text for words part of a character's natural speech to build authenticity (like Spanish in a Latinx character's dialogue), using italics primarily to distinguish truly unfamiliar terms or to avoid misreading as typos, and noting that frequently used words might only need italics on the first mention." The author

opted for regular text for all instances, except when emphasis is implied as part of speech.

Italic use on English words in conversation are spoken in Italian or the Galluric dialect and other Sardo dialects common to Sardinia (known as a "Romanza Insulare" - a Latin branch of its own separate from Italian) indicate what the character (commonly Mario) understands and is represented using grammatically-correct English phrasing, not the literal phrasing that was common during the Modernist literary movement. Some author liberty is taken with this as well.

3. If you're curious where some of the reference material is for Sardo (the language) is feel free to wade through the references listed here:

CaliaWilde.com/language

THE HUNTERS' CODE

The Thumb: Life
    (The Grip and Foundation)
    Live by the code.
    Live with purpose.
    Live with clarity.
    Life is the reward.

The Index Finger: Honor
    (The Direction and Guide)
    Honor the code.
    Honor every marker.
    Honor the family.
    Honor rewards itself

The Middle Finger: Discipline
    (The Spine and Trade)
    Finish the job.

Eliminate complications.
Deceive wisely.
Guard your secrets.

The Ring Finger: Respect
(The Vow to Elements)
Respect the sea.
Respect your elders.
Respect your home.
Cherish innocence.

The Pinky: Death
(The End/Finality)
Die by the code.
Die with dignity.
Die without regret.
Death is your gift.

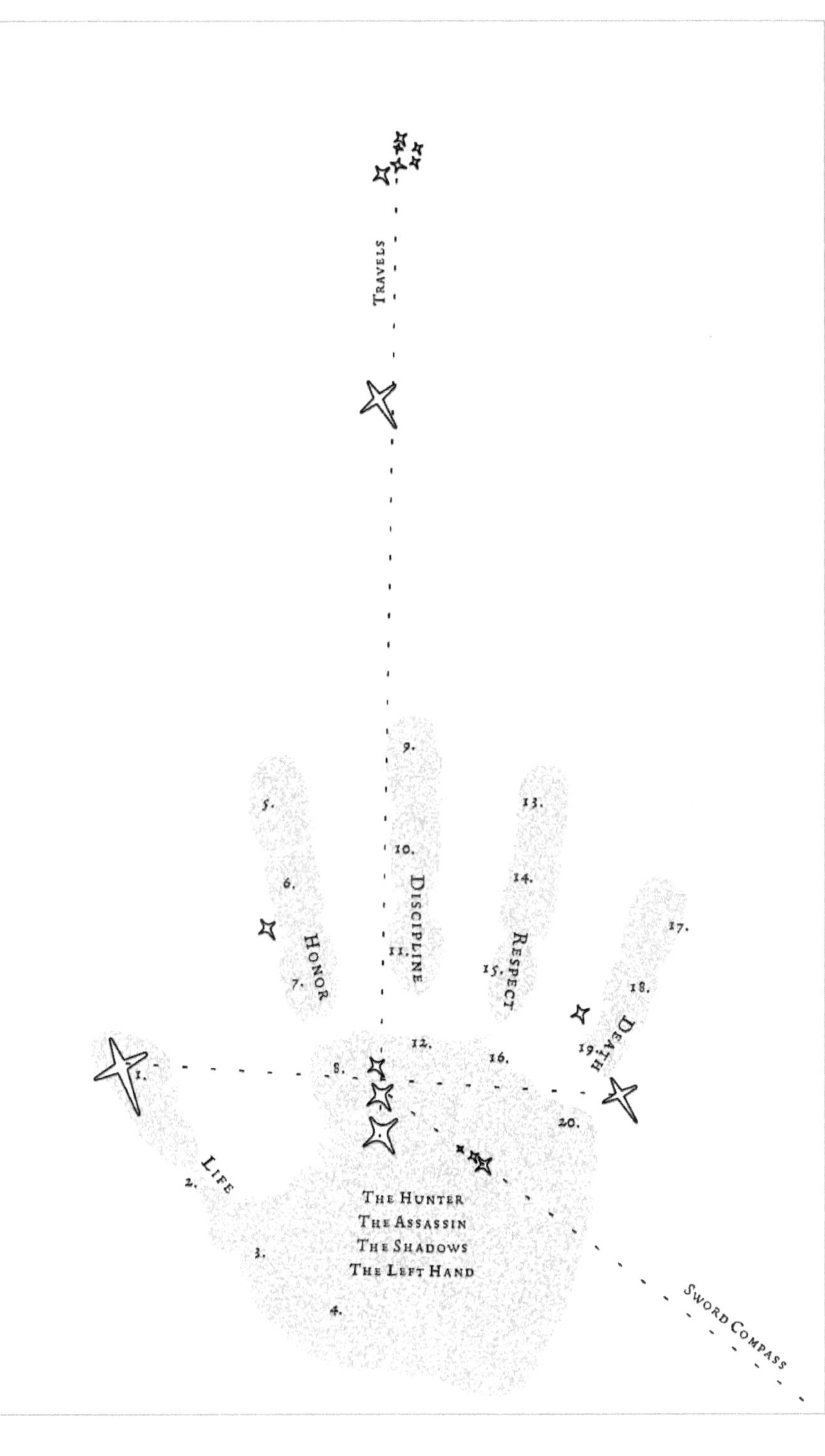

Travels
Discipline
Honor
Respect
Death
Life
Sword Compass
The Hunter
The Assassin
The Shadows
The Left Hand
1.
2.
3.
4.
5.
6.
7.
8.
9.
10.
11.
12.
13.
14.
15.
16.
17.
18.
19.
20.

To the PI sprint group members.

Thank you for listening to this crazy cast of characters and putting up with all the plot bunnies hopping around.

VALENTINE'S CODE

1

MARIO

The contract on my head was worth seven million dollars as of two minutes ago. Like any Vegas odds sheet, that number went up with each unsuccessful hit. I'd eluded at least two in the last twenty-four hours. My need for an ally, or a dozen of them, lured me to the City of Sin, home to various organized crime figures, and my last resort to evade my executioners.

On the tarmac of McCarran International, a private jet was being prepped. It was one of the family's seven business fleet aircraft ranging from the luxurious to the ridiculous. A certain internet celebrity bought our biggest one four years ago. We'd replaced it with an even larger one.

How else were we supposed to keep up with the global demands of organized crime?

I sipped my cognac and pondered the logistics. That's what I did best. Logistics. From meetings to murder, I was the most glorified administrative assistant to the oldest of monied mobsters in Europe and beyond. They relied upon me. So, it was absurd I'd be fingered for a hit, right?

I sighed and took another sip of my drink. Even paper pushers had their enemies. The devil was always in the details often overlooked by the incautious.

"You're hiding in plain sight."

Speaking of his royal darkness … "Ringo. I'd ask what you're doing here, but ... I take it you're working?" Ringo Devlin was one of the best hitmen in the business. I should know; I helped arrange almost every one of his kills. They went flawlessly thanks to his ruthless cunning and my expert planning.

"I've got five minutes before I start." My best friend since boarding school signaled to the bartender for a drink. The Macallan 18 bottle looked dusty despite the glittering lights and neon distractions surrounding us.

"You took the contract, didn't you?"

Ringo snorted into his drink. "Of course."

"If you need money—"

He held a finger up. "I'd've asked. But I'm not doing it for the money. Although, seven million…"

It would finally pay off his debt on a folly. And with me gone, he'd have that post-modern Italian ocean-view monstrosity to himself. But knowing him, that would last all of one day before he found a woman to splash naked in the little atrium fountain located in the foyer leading to the terrace overlook.

His roving eye trailed a prospective conquest in a practically see-through gown as she rushed through the lobby. The bottom hem of the flesh-pink gauze trailed along the carpet like a cloud.

"… the money would be enough of an incentive for most." He continued on, still tracking the woman.

"How are you going to do it?"

He snapped his attention to me. "Who do you think I am? If I tell you that, you'll figure out ten different ways to stop me."

"It would make the job far more interesting." I dangled my words like bait.

He sipped his drink, pondering my statement. "I think it would."

"It's not like you're going to really kill me."

"Oh, now there's where you are wrong, my friend. I can and will kill you. The way I figure it, it better be me rather than some idiot trying to make a name for themselves."

True. "Make it quick." I glanced up at the security camera embedded into the mirrored surface of the ceiling. Ringo wouldn't do it here. He'd had to have spotted it.

He scoffed. "I'm not an amateur."

That he wasn't.

He turned back to crowd watching. "You know, you're lucky."

I was? He ignored my scowl and kept talking.

"Anyone else would have made this messy."

"Like it's not?"

His head tip was not reassuring. I knew Ringo well enough that he'd just dismissed my warnings and started down his own unique brand of mayhem. "You know your problem, Valentine?"

It was Valentini, but he'd been calling me by the bastardized version of my patronymic since we were eight, so I dismissed the slight and focused my attention to whatever bullshit was going to spout from his mouth next. "I suppose you're going to tell me."

"Damn straight. You live like you're dying."

That didn't make sense. "Everyone dies."

He grunted as if to acknowledge the truth, but carried on. "But if you live like that, it isn't really living, is it? Take *that* for an incentive."

That being the woman in the sheer dress. She'd joined a strikingly similar woman in an almost equally sheer wedding dress. Both women were blonde, tall, model-thin, yet refreshingly wholesome. The one who wore the nude pink gown wore little to no makeup. Her lean face had intriguing angles and possessed a bold nose. Her eyes were a shade of medium color I'd guess as green or hazel but it was hard to tell from this distance. The other was in profile, addressing her wren-like twin with grand gestures and a sway that indicated she was drunk.

Very drunk. Not the first bride to indulge before or after her nuptials. This was Vegas, after all. Perhaps she'd been jilted at the altar? And perhaps her bridesmaid twin was consoling her? Or at least, appeasing her.

Yes, that was what was happening. The more beautiful twin had that stance. She leaned in as if to catch the woman should her sway turn into a slump. Both of her hands were poised to catch. I knew that position well. Ringo was a double handful. And if he were drunk, a whole airbus of hands full.

"The women?" I clarified. Ringo could be talking about something else.

"Twins, man. Do you know what you could do with twins?" He tapped the bar surface emphasizing his words, then sucked in his bottom lip and bit it theatrically.

"We," I corrected. One was all I wanted to explore at a time, and seeing as they were sisters and likely to talk, one would be all I'd explore if I were even inclined to do so. Two would be… Ringo's style, not mine.

The side-eye he shot me was filled with disgust. "I swear you were born with that stick up your ass."

"It's a code, not a stick." Honor was a rare thing meant to be upheld with the utmost sobriety and gravity it deserved.

"Your code is going to get you killed. I knew you'd be here doing things by the book. That damn code…"

The women were arguing. One tugging the other toward the slot machines, and the other fighting her and pointing the way toward the exit. Who would win?

"The code has kept me alive." Not an easy feat when your family was as notorious as mine.

"Well, this time it screwed you."

Appeasing my father screwed me. Faking interest in that she-devil was an insult. But one I'd now have to swallow to keep the peace. "I'll fix it."

Ringo was silent. I'd expected him to laugh.

"You don't believe me?"

He took a deep breath. "Listen, I've known you for… Jesus, twenty-five years. And you can be a real martyr sometimes, but I've never known you to be *stupid*. Dianora Conti? Jesus."

"It's not stupid, it's politics."

Ringo squared off with me. "Marrying the black widow of Tuscany is *not* politics, it's suicide."

That it was. But it was the only way I'd survive to see next year. And surviving was rule number one of the code. Second was honoring your family. I'd manage both if I could lie well enough.

Lying to family was against the code. I hadn't done that, yet.

Marrying someone I didn't love was accepted in the circles I ran in. It didn't matter that it was against my *personal* code.

Protecting my grandfather from disgrace? Absolutely in the code.

"If I don't accept her offer, you'll have to go through with your contract. Or someone will. And if you fail, they'll kill you."

"I don't fucking care, Val. If someone else gets to you first, I *should* be dead. And, honestly? I'd want to die anyway. You're the best, and I'm not just talking logistically. The best friend, the best criminal mastermind, and a much better man than I am."

"Then why did you take the hit? You could have saved yourself a lot of trouble."

He stared at me.

"What?"

"I could give you a bunch of reasons, but I guess the biggest one is this: I want to do it because you're the best.

When I do this? I'll never have to work again. They'll never ask me to do anything harder. I guarantee that."

The alcohol I'd sipped churned in my gut. He was serious.

And if he failed, and if I managed to convince Dianora Conti to marry me for my family's power, and by doing so, force her father to remove the price on my head, Ringo would be the next one with a hit on his head. Because she earned her nickname of Black Widow. Ringo wouldn't be the only victim. She'd get bored of me eventually. Perhaps I'd live long enough to sire an heir on her, but life as I knew it was over. And *anyone* who called me friend would be dead, or wish they were.

I'd sign Ringo's death warrant by wiggling out of the hit.

I glanced at my watch. It had been five minutes. The sober sister won the argument, dragging the drunken bride to the door. And the world was righting itself. "For what it's worth? I didn't kill Adelmo Conti." I stood up and opened my arms wide so Ringo would have a clean shot.

He glared at me. "I'm not doing you here. You have one minute to walk out that door and prove to me you're the best in the business."

I stood still, the countdown automatically ticking down in my head. "How are you going to do it?"

Ringo slammed his drink and licked his lips. Then returned to staring me down. His lips pressed into a silent line of focus.

On twenty I took a step away. Then another step.

By ten I was halfway to the exit and Ringo still stood

next to the bar. He pulled out his wallet and laid a bill on the surface for the bartender, as if this were just a normal day.

It was anything but.

On zero, I stepped out of the doors into the night air and beelined for the strip. Vegas in all its glory glittered around me. Traffic bustled, street hawkers littered the constant stream of tourists and gawkers like the little pamphlets they dropped.

Cabs and black limos waited near the hotel's circle. I stepped forward to take the next one in line, but I was shoved to the side by a wide man in a polyester suit. "That's my ride, and I'm late for my flight."

If I were carrying, I'd knife the bastard for that.

Ringo emerged from the entrance. His slow saunter, sure-footed and direct. I slipped into the crowds moving toward the fountains, staying agile and slightly outpacing the flow. I took the stairs to the walkway, crossed north, and kept moving.

I entered another casino and cut through their maze of slot machines, hoping to catch a ride at their cab stand before Ringo or another hitman beat me to it. Once there, I would direct the driver to the company's private airport and then—

A man peeled off the casino's column. He approached me with all the subtly of a wallowing hippo. The bulge of his concealed gun was obvious. I stopped, waiting for him in a little alcove where the security cameras couldn't watch.

Ringo approached from the side, barely a shadow.

How had he outflanked me?

He brushed past, elbowing me out of the way and knocking the man into the alcove. Ringo's victim collapsed into a lump and didn't move.

I stepped out of arm's reach. My friend winked at me and mouthed, "That's one."

Bastard. Instead of lingering there like a sitting duck, I hopped the escalator up one floor, then crossed to the pedestrian walkway that dumped me on the opposite side of the strip. I dipped into a hotel, moving toward the shops. There was a ride share loop just off the strip. Perhaps I could steal one of the rides as easily as I'd been thwarted earlier. I was halfway down the escalator when Ringo ran up from the street. I hopped over the rail to the stairs and ran back up. Ringo ran up the escalator, almost beating me to the top. I pointed at the security camera mounted in its little black bubble on the ceiling and cut left. Instead of turning toward the shops, I took the escalator up to the monorail. At the top, I took a quick right into the parking garage hallway.

Ringo was hot on my tail. No matter how much I zigged and zagged, he stuck close. I was almost to the stairs when he caught me and pulled me between two large SUVs.

I had nowhere left to run. There I stood, hands in the air, puffing hard, staring at my best friend since before either of us could shave, knowing he was going to kill me.

There was nothing left but to barter for my life. "You're going to hate yourself when you figure out who murdered Dianora's brother, because it wasn't me."

Ringo pocketed his gun. "Who did it?"

I rushed him, knocking him hard and climbing over top

of his falling body. As I cleared him, I turned to tell him, "I don't know. But I didn't do it."

His hand shot out.

A flare of hot pain sliced through my abdomen, sending me in a staggering rush backward. I almost fell on my ass but managed to keep my feet under me.

Then I ran.

My best friend, practically my *only* friend, stabbed me.

Game on.

2

ALLIE

Some days I wished I could have been born an only child to a completely different family. Don't get me wrong, I love my family, but they have their share of skeletons in the proverbial closet. I also love my sister, Ellie. She's the best twin a person could have. But she had a nasty habit of lying her way into horribly complicated fiascos.

Today's was the worst one yet. We were in Las Vegas for an obvious reason, her quickie wedding to one Johnny Porciello. Or as I'd taken to calling him, Johnny Pornstash. Because that mustache had to go.

Of course, without it, he'd look like a pre-teen.

Johnny was thirty-one years old and had the baby-soft skin of a fourteen-year-old, and just about as much facial hair, except for that dreadful caterpillar on his upper lip. It was as if his body had something to prove, but was incapable of doing more. In more ways than that, he was unworthy of my baby sister.

I was thirteen minutes older, therefore wiser, or something like that. Even though wisdom wasn't magically bestowed through those thirteen minutes, I still knew this marriage was a bad idea.

And while putting on our dresses that afternoon, Ellie walked through the doorway of reality, finally, and realized it was an unquestionably awful idea to marry Johnny Pornstach. Which spiraled into a very bad evening.

Tequila should not be consumed before five in the afternoon. Especially not by brides who just found out their soon-to-be-husband was a lowlife, gangsta' wannabe fresh out of his mother's basement.

It all started because I'd gotten a tip. Not the cash kind, the clandestine kind.

Normally, I'd completely ignore anything that came from my maternal grandfather's lawyer because it was bound to be tied up in so many strings it would make the Gordian knot look like child's play. But this was hand-delivered by the hotel concierge himself with an urgent demand of, "Please make your sister look at the contents of this package. My Boss insists." Capital B, *Boss*.

I ripped the envelope open, expecting to find yet another court summons to fight the challenges to my grandfather's estate, and instead got a handful of photos of Johnny's wrecked Mustang.

It was mangled beyond the point of repair. In the background was a Mercedes that didn't look much better. In fact, it looked much worse. Johnny had rammed into the driver's side so hard the steering column was in the middle of the vehicle.

Luxury automobile or not, whoever was in that car wasn't walking away.

Clipped to the top photo was a hand-written note.

"The Family needs to be notified. If your sister goes through with this wedding, there will be a price."

Crap. Family. Capital F. Not the family of the victim. That's not how this lawyer worked. He wasn't asking for more money, he was warning us that whoever Johnny hit with that car was likely "connected." Just like my dear departed grandfather was connected. Just like the owners of this hotel were connected to a friend of a friend of someone who had a friend who knew a guy, ya know?

My family secret wasn't a secret to that crowd. It was a legend. One that, two generations later, made accomplished men grovel like a puppy who'd just peed on your shoes. Unlike the puppy, I didn't have an explanation why humans did things like that.

If I thought Chicago was a cesspool, Vegas was the whole damn sewage treatment plant.

And for an accountant, my grandfather had lived a very *interesting* life. So interesting, the FBI were my neighbors until I graduated from college and started my post graduate studies in veterinary sciences. No matter how straight and narrow my immediate family lived, they were interesting, too. But monitoring a veterinary surgeon was too boring for the feds, and I finally lived like a normal person, with a normal job, like every other law-abiding citizen.

That was until *the will*.

Ugh.

And the press… which ruined everyone's lives. Mom

and Dad took a settlement, an early retirement, and fled to Arizona with a matched pair of alpacas, their collection of tie-dyed shirts, and a used school bus where they'd live happily ever after out of the spotlight. Meanwhile, I lost my career. No one wanted to hire the mob heiress. That would be too risky.

Ellie? Well, cocktail waitressing at a dive bar on the outskirts of the Chicago suburbs wasn't the type of job that rumor and criminal underworld entanglement exactly hurt. In fact, she turned the notoriety into better tips because "she knew a guy, ya know?"

And that's where Johnny Pornstash fell in love—with my little sister's trust fund and the lure of mob connections.

Except we weren't connected. Not one bit.

She was blind, thinking him a harmless thug. It was the baby face that had fooled her, I was certain of it.

Thank God, she caught me red-handed with the goods. I passed them off to her with a warning, "You need to think about this wedding, hard."

"Is that an order, Doctor Stickupherass?"

It was. "Jaja's lawyer said it, I didn't. Read the note clipped to the top photo."

Her face paled. "Did you look at any of these?"

"Not unless you won't. We finally got free of **FBI** surveillance, and I for one don't want to go back to that life. Remember how they frisked our prom dates?"

Ellie made a guttural gagging noise at the memory. "Assholes."

I wouldn't go quite that far, but they had made our lives pretty miserable. Growing up like that sent me down a path of buttoning every button, planning to the point of obsession, and never, ever, putting even the tip of a big toe over the line.

Ellie?

That's all she ever did. Toes, heels, whole legs…

She flipped through the photos and got to about the fourth one before her knees got wobbly and she fell faster than a soufflé. I couldn't even catch her before she became a sparkly, chiffon and crystal-beaded puddle on the floor.

My sister couldn't stand the sight of blood.

And there was a lot of it in that photo.

Some bullet holes, too.

Johnny was a lot more awful than a reckless driver.

I shoved the photos with their clipped-on note into my suitcase and got out the smelling salts.

Ellie woke up with a groan and a mission labeled, "drink that man right out of mind."

Which meant the afternoon tequila binge, and missing the chapel limo. The latter arrived precisely on time to collect the back-up dresses my sister bought, Ellie's carry-on, and my stocked tote bag before it whisked away, right according to plan. Except the delivery was devoid of one bride and one bridesmaid because I was busy looking for Ellie at the hotel bar.

There were *eleven* to search. But I lucked out and found her at number three. She was easy to spot in her wedding gown.

"Oh. My. God, Allie, what are we going to do? The mob is going to come after us."

What's this 'us' thing you're talking about? "They're not. If they go after anybody, they'll go after Johnny. You're not marrying him, remember?" I was being supportive. Or as supportive as I could get wearing a practically see-through bridesmaid dress almost the same color as my skin. Sure, I suppose it was pretty for a supermodel, or an actress trying to shake a child-star fanbase, but for an out-of-work veterinarian still in therapy from the trauma caused by the panopticon of my childhood? Hell to the no.

It looked like lingerie.

The funny thing about it was that barely anyone noticed. Their eyes were on Ellie in her beautiful, sparkly wedding dress. Random people would walk up and say, 'Congratulations,' then smile and look around for the villainous and missing groom. At first, I smiled and tried to say 'thank you' while squeezing Ellie's hand so she'd not blurt out something horrible. But after she smacked me in the shoulder for getting too rough, I gave up.

Then things got much more interesting.

"Oh, you're getting married. Congratulations!" The couple must have been pushing one-fifty, collectively.

"Fuck off with that shit, my fiancé is a no-good amateur murderer, and once I find his ass, he'll get an education on how murders *should* be done."

Their eyes went wide, and they shuffled away.

"That tops the culinary school threat."

Ellie shrugged. "If I chopped Johnny into pieces, there's bound to be blood. I'd faint again and ruin this dress." She picked at the heavily boned and beaded corset. "And I *love* this dress. But, do you think I should have worn the other one?"

She bought *two* wedding dresses with matching bridesmaid ensembles. This one was stunning, featuring a flat-front bodice with pearl and sequin embellishments reminiscent of the 1600s, along with a draped tulle skirt. It gathered at Ellie's hip. The excess cascaded from the focal point in tiers. The designer embellished each delicate layer with crystals sewn into the fabric so artfully it sparkled like a waterfall that extended to the train's end. Ellie glittered under the lights of the ride share pavilion I'd led her to.

My dress didn't have sequins. It looked like the whorehouse version that should layer under that dress. "You're not getting married anymore, remember?"

She sighed heavily. "What a waste of a dress. I wish I'd worn the other one. It would have been so pretty."

The other one was the opera lingerie one. It had a matching bridesmaid dress that wasn't even legal it was so see-through. Thank God it was in the limo or at the chapel because I talked Allie into trying these on first.

Not that the wedding gown she'd picked to match that abomination was much better. Her alternate dress was completely sheer with a keyhole window that touched her bellybutton. If not for all the off the shoulder bodice ruffles and its numerous flower appliqués, it would be indecent even for Vegas.

Ellie spun in a circle and mused, "They're both cursed now." She fluffed the train so it fell in a perfect little curve at her feet.

"They can't be cursed because you didn't get married in them." *When would that driver get here?* I checked my phone to discover the little icon of the car was still idling two blocks away. Were we supposed to go there? No, the hotel was very clear that ride shares could not pick people up on the Strip. That made logistical sense, so I didn't question it.

"I'm going back to change."

"No!" I grabbed her arm and begged her to stay still. "We're just going to go to the chapel, get the deposit back, and pick up our things, then we can change, or whatever you want, but please don't leave me here alone." *And please don't make me hunt you down again.*

"Oh Allie, you gotta lighten up. The world is an okay place. Live a little for a change. I swear you believe everyone is out to murder you."

Tell that to the homeless guy sleeping on the bench across the street.

Wait, if he was sleeping, that meant he was safe, so… was Ellie technically right? I pondered that for a half-second. "I know you *think* it's safe, it's just that I want to stick together, okay?" *So you don't do something stupid like spend your entire trust fund on a spare-no-expense wedding excursion with nothing to show for it.* I gritted out a smile that I hoped was kind.

"Your face is going to stick that way." She tossed her perfectly styled hair back. "We could take the monorail. That sounds like fun."

"It stops running at midnight, and only goes halfway there." I'd checked the schedule and route five times.

Ellie, being enamored with all things cursed, chose midnight of February 13 to get married. Although technically I guess the "I-do's" would be on Valentine's Day, right? Another thing I put off pondering until I shut down this shit show carnival ride. There would be no Valentine's Day or Valentine's Day-eve wedding.

"Oh. No monorail. Okay. I'm going back to the hotel. Allie, do you worst with the deposit. Whatever you keep is yours. Here's the plane tickets, the license, everything. I don't care anymore." She handed off my carefully compiled binder.

"Ellie, *no*. We're going to Italy tomorrow…together, remember?" I'd talked her into it after she announced the wedding was off. I needed the license and the chapel information but shoved the plane tickets back in her hand so she'd have something tangible to remind her not to go on another bender. "Hang onto these for me."

My drunk sister stared at the night sky. "Fuck. The very last thing I want to do is fly right now."

The flight was *hours* from now. But I couldn't tell her that. "Ellie, please? Just stay with me. It won't take long, I promise." As soon as she offered the ticket change, I jumped. I needed something to get my mind off my unemployment situation. And Italy? That was a fantastical dream of mine. It was maybe even a guilty little secret ambition I'd harbored ever since one of the FBI neighbors let slip that my jaja was in the mob. I just knew once I landed in Italy, I'd be revered as the mafia princess I was born to be. I had such an imagination at six.

I should have known Pulaski was not an Italian surname.

Ellie squared up in front of me. "Big sis, I love you, but here's the deal, I'm drunk and starting to get sober. Your idea of something not taking long and mine are two completely different things. If we have any chance at all of pulling off this fake honeymoon excursion together, I *need* sleep. And I'll even sweeten the deal. I'll go back to the hotel to pack the rest of our stuff and sleep this off. Someone has to, otherwise we'll be up all night. So, let me do that. Then we'll ride to the airport in the morning as early as you want."

I hesitated.

"I know you think I can't pack."

She couldn't. At least not effectively. Ellie had a tendency to pack by clothing type. Which meant she could have one whole bag only filled with swimsuits. What if the other bags got lost?

She rushed on, oblivious to my thoughts. "And I know you had to chase me down this afternoon, but I vow, I won't do anything stupid now. Trust me."

"You'll pack *everything*?"

She stared at me with that look on her face I'd grown to dread. Like I'd kicked her puppy.

"Allie, I can do this. I just have to get back to the hotel, pack all the shit in the room, zonk out until you get back, then you'll take over, and we're golden."

Well, that was a solid enough start. When did she become the planner?

"Sounds good," I quickly said before she could change her mind.

As she stumbled away, I heard her say, "Cursed. This dress is cursed. Such a shame. I look hot in it."

"It's not cursed!"

She was already moving up the escalator, but flipped me the bird as she rose upward like some demonic angel on a mission. "For the record, I was a beautiful bride!" she shouted to the sky.

And the car was moving, *finally*. Maybe Ellie's dress was cursed, and I'd just been freed from its sphere of influence? Ponder later, act now. I searched the street for the color and model listed in the app. When it came into sight, I started waving my arms like a madwoman.

The driver of the black car spotted me and pulled into the curved circle where I waited. I had just opened the door and greeted him when out of nowhere a man in a suit stumbled into me and rolled into the back seat where *I* should be. I'd barely pushed him away in time to avoid getting plowed over.

"Hey!"

He stared at me with wide eyes.

Pretty, brown eyes, with thick lashes and… damn it.

"This is my car," I said, lamely.

Instead of doing the right thing and getting out or apologizing, he pulled the door shut then leaned forward and somehow convinced the driver to take off without me.

"Jerk!" I screamed into the night air.

"Where'd he go?"

The man asking was a little rough and breathless. His black shirt was torn, and there was a scuffed point on one knee that ruined the lines of his expensive slacks. With his five o'clock shadow and the wild mess of his surfer-highlighted brownish-red hair, he was everything Ellie would drool over. Rich clothes, wild appearance, and an attitude. Me? I was unaffected to say the least. "The fucking wedding chapel, I hope. Serves him right taking my car." I tapped away on the app to report the issue and hired a new ride.

"Which wedding chapel?"

I glared at an interruption made flesh. He was being nosy, and kind of rude. I wasn't in a charitable mood. "What are you going to do, hunt him down and kill him for me?"

A slow grin spread across his face. "For you? Absolutely. And, I'd do it for free." His eyes dipped southward.

Next, he'd start drooling. *Ugh.*

I quickly covered the sheer places of my corset where the strapless bra barely hid my nipples between the slats of ribboned boning. "Eyes up. That's a lame pick up line."

The grin hadn't faded. "Apologies, I see a beautiful woman and sometimes I can't help it."

"Try."

That made his smirk fall. "Is your twin as evil as you are?"

How did he know I had a twin?

He took a step back with both hands up, as if to give me space, or avoid getting hit. "Wow. That question on your face is deadly. And you don't have to ask me how I know. I saw you two at the casino." He pointed across the street. "You're both very pretty. That's all. And her being a bride, just…"

…attracted attention, I got it. "Well, she's not going to be a bride today. Cold feet." That was a nice way to phrase it. Better than dismembered corpses and various murder plots.

Whoever he was, he had the decency to straighten the hopeful quirk of his mouth. "I'm… sorry?"

Why did that sound like a question?

I pointed in the direction my ride share had disappeared with his quarry safely ensconced in the back seat. "Listen, I was going to straighten out the no-show at the chapel, retrieve our things, and hopefully get a refund. If the car drops him off there, you *can* kill him for me." I rattled off the name and address of the wedding chapel.

"Thank you."

Instead of sticking around, he dodged back into the parking garage.

"Weirdo."

My ride share arrived. This time I got in before anyone could snag it. So much for safety first.

As I settled back and plotted my next moves, I rubbed at something sticky on my fingers. It had smeared onto my phone as well.

Bits of brown dust flaked off where the substance had dried. I powered up my phone screen and almost screamed, but managed to keep my terror quiet.

The driver was oblivious to my predicament.

There was blood on my hands and my dress.

3

MARIO

The driver didn't appreciate the knife I'd stolen from Ringo. Holding it at his throat probably didn't help. To appease him, I offered him a hundred dollars to cancel the prior ride and take me to the airport.

My mistake.

Instead of driving south, he drove north.

"Where are you going?"

"I have to go to the programmed destination."

"No, you don't. You canceled it."

"Please, mister? Don't kill me." His hands were shaking.

Logistically, Ringo would expect me to divert the car to the airport. "Fine." I'd find another ride from wherever this car landed. I'd have to plan how to avoid him when I got to the private flight hangar. I had a knife. Would I need more than that? Naw. I'd disarmed Ringo without even thinking.

"Thank you so much, I mean, for not robbing me or killing me, or—"

"Shut up and I'll give you an extra fifty. Not one word, got it?"

He nodded quickly and zipped down the side streets to avoid the traffic on the strip. There was still a bottleneck by the convention center, and another delay as we passed the Stratosphere. I squinted at the road ahead. The only things up here were strip clubs and… wedding chapels.

Right. Her sister was getting married.

I felt awful now.

Well, more awful. Ringo nicked me good. I'd soaked through my shirt, and the expensive Italian wool suit jacket I wore was working overtime to absorb the blood. At this rate, I'd bleed out before I left Las Vegas.

The driver pulled into one of the larger wedding chapel complexes. The billboard overhead advertised complete wedding packages, including on-site tuxedo rentals and costumes for themed events. I handed off the fifty and got out.

Out of habit, I scanned the area for resources.

Across the street was a tattoo parlor. They would have antiseptic and gauze. I looked both ways and crossed.

The artist on duty took my cash, handed over what I asked for without questions, and let me use their restroom. After wrapping the wound, I could maneuver much better. Luckily, it wasn't as bad as it looked. I'd survive. I just needed clean clothes. Preferably something without branding on it that would make me stick out in the exclusive airport lounge.

And I knew just the place. I prepared to cross the street again.

Right as I did, two things happened. First, a dog walker lost their grip on their diminutive Yorkie who got spooked by a motorcycle and sprinted ahead of me, and second, a gray sedan arrived at the chapel. Ringo stepped out of it.

The stupid dog ran straight at my nemesis. But the traffic on the strip was faster than its little legs could move. It froze right in the middle of a lane of oncoming traffic. The owner screamed for help. I ran into the road, scooped up the dog, and sprinted the last bit of distance giving me the momentum to dive into the parking lot, cradling the bundle of fluff as I hit the pavement where I rolled to a stop at Ringo's feet.

"Here." I jumped up, handed him the dog, and slipped inside the wedding complex. That should keep his hands busy for a few moments.

Just before the glass doors behind me slid shut, the dog's owner offered Ringo money for his heroic rescue.

He'd have to decline, then they'd argue over it, buying me two minutes while I found a place to hide. Excellent. Another plan sorted and executed without a hitch.

The garden chapel was too exposed. The main chapel, not much better. It was all decked out like a gaudy renaissance castle complete with fog machine and guards flanking the fake royal officiant. I wound deeper into the complex and checked doors. The second door I tried was a large storage room or grandiose closet filled with costumes of every shape, size, and color. *Score.* I wouldn't even have to talk to anyone.

I searched through the racks. Tuxedos, suits, costumes…

I had my pick of the lot. I chose black in case the bandage I'd put on leaked. Rolling across asphalt hadn't helped any. I tightened the bandages and slipped on a fresh pair of pants and shirt. There was a matching cape with red lining on the hanger. With it, hung a cheesy, white half-mask. I wouldn't need that, but took it anyway so I could slip through the hallways undetected.

The door opened, and I slid behind the racks, hiding from the trio of actors who'd just wrapped up the royal wedding.

"That's almost the last show of the night." One of the royal guards said.

"Thank goodness. My feet are killing me," said a woman who slipped out of a maiden's costume and immediately into a white gown with elaborate flowers sewn across the bodice and skirt. The officiate rummaged through the racks.

The second guard popped his head in the room. "Hey, has anyone seen the next bride? We've got the groom waiting, and the feed goes live in ten minutes."

The officiate answered him. "She texted that she's running late. Ride share issues."

Whoops. That was on me.

He searched the rack I was hiding behind. I stayed excruciatingly still so he wouldn't see me.

"Has anyone seen my phantom costume?"

I glanced at the white mask peeking out from under the heavy cape in my hand.

"There's one over here."

"I could have sworn I hung mine by the door. Oh, well.

If the bride doesn't show, I won't need it. Can you help me with my wig?"

Two of the actors moved to the makeup area and the smell of solvent permeated the air. The door opened again. "The bride's here. She's meeting with the event organizer. It might not happen, folks."

"Oh, thank the Gods. Valentine's Day and the night before it are the fucking worst." Guard one dropped his outfit on a stool, abandoning his costume change.

"It pays the bills," the woman commented as she pulled the wig off the king's head and rubbed at a stray patch of glue.

"Fuck staying. Tomorrow is going to be a killer. It will be fifteen hours of wedding insanity. I'm out."

"Me too. Good luck with the Bridezilla."

The two guards who'd spoken changed into street clothes. The woman and the officiate stayed behind, still working on the glue residue left behind by his elaborate wig.

I took a chance and slipped out of the area before someone else trapped me here.

Outside the room, I donned the opera mask and cape, pulling the stiff collar up to conceal the unmasked side of my face.

"Jerry! Room three. I need you."

A woman stood in the hallway, holding the door open and frantically motioning inside. Reluctantly, I followed directions and went inside.

"Thanks! I'll be right back; I've got to go collect the groom. She wants a refund. See if you can fix this, okay?" The door shut behind me before I could protest.

I turned around to see who "Jerry" was supposed to talk to. It was her. The twin to the bride, and the ride share requestor I'd almost flattened before I stole her ride.

"*You.*"

Her voice dripped acid.

"I'm… sorry?"

"Oh, you're not sorry yet." She stood up, her hands fisted.

"I can explain."

"Can it. I just want my money back."

My mouth opened and shut. "For the ride?" I could afford thirty dollars easily.

She waved that off. "No, they refunded it. For the wedding."

I squinted at her outfit. She clutched a folder close rather than setting it down. "Where's the bride?"

"Hopefully back at the hotel, packing. Thank goodness she's showing some initiative. I swear this whole trip was cursed."

Awkward silence followed her outburst. "I can't help you with a refund." I needed to leave.

"Oh, I know that. You're just some rando, who… Why are you dressed like that?"

Uh… because I was bleeding? "I…work here?"

"Nice try. Tell it to someone who isn't allergic to BS."

The door opened at my back and I stifled the urge to stab the newcomer. The woman who'd ushered me into the room shoved a young man in a tuxedo over the threshold, then ordered everyone to, and I quote, "Work this shit out. I've got a Clark County Marriage License Bureau Justice outside insisting on watching this one *personally*. We *can't* cancel!"

The door slammed behind her.

"Ellie—" the newcomer started to say.

"Allie!" she corrected.

"Oh shit, my bad. Where's Ellie?"

"I'm not telling *you* because you're *not* marrying my sister."

"But Allie, she *has* to. You heard the wedding planner, a fucking judge is out there." He took a threatening step forward, crowding Allie.

I jumped into the breach, placing a hand on his chest to push him away. "Mind yourself."

"Who the fuck are you?"

Given my costume, it was amusing to say, "Your worst nightmare."

Unfortunately, it didn't have the same effect on this peon as it did on people who knew who I was.

"Whoop-dee-do. This is between me and Ellie."

"Allie." She didn't yell this time, but the warning bite in her tone was clear.

"Whatever. I'm getting married to *one* of you women tonight whether you like it or not."

"Excuse me?" I said, inserting myself between them further.

At the same time, Allie said, "Over my dead body."

"That can be arranged." Idiot boy tried to shove me aside to get at the woman.

I stopped his progress by twisting his arm behind his

back. He fought it, of course. Meanwhile, I asked Allie, "How dead do you want him?"

She stared at me as if weighing my question seriously. "Dead enough to not get up for at least two to maybe five hours, but not dead-dead. I don't want to be arrested in this dress."

"Done." I hit the boy on the back of the skull with the butt of Ringo's knife. It was hard enough to drop him. Hopefully, it wasn't hard enough to cause brain damage, but he'd definitely wake up with a concussion.

"Wow. You were serious."

"I'm always serious." To a fault, according to Ringo.

Speaking of the devil, I heard his voice outside charming the wedding planner. Another voice joined theirs, older and deeper.

I straightened my mask and quickly turned so my profile was hidden by the costume. I chanced a look in the room's large standing mirror and caught sight of Ringo before the door closed, placing me, the older man and the wedding planner inside with Allie.

"What happened to the groom?!" The planner pointed at the unconscious imbecile.

"I clobbered him when he threatened me." Allie jumped to my defense quickly. That would not do. I opened my mouth to correct her, but the wedding planner jumped all over me.

"And you just let her? Damn it, Jerry."

I took off my mask. "I'm not Jerry."

Her jaw dropped.

Allie's notably, didn't.

The older man slapped his hands together. "Oh, you must be the Eye-talian our little Ellie is marrying."

Allie opened her mouth to say "Allie," but I sent her a warning glance over the man's shoulder.

"You have me at a loss, sir." I held out a friendly hand to distract him from the barely breathing body in the corner.

"Oh, shoot, I'm Judge Stone, Oliver Stone, like that movie guy, you know the one. I'm the Justice of the Peace around here. And I owe little Ellie's late grandfather a favor so I thought to oversee this one *personally*. Did you know he signed off for the funds on the Sunrise Hospital himself?" Oliver pumped my arm like the seasoned politician he was. I smiled convincingly and kept an eye on Allie who was gearing up to say something that would straighten the whole situation out.

"Charmed."

Allie sent me the stink-eye.

"But who's this? I thought he was the groom." The wedding planner pointed at the man-baby sleeping in the corner.

Allie answered, "That's Johnny. Ellie's *ex*-boyfriend…for a good reason."

The wedding planner turned red. "Oh. I'm so sorry, he shouldn't be in here. Maybe I should find a doctor or something?"

"You do that, little lady. I'm going to make sure the papers are all buttoned up here."

The Justice stayed behind as the wedding planner dragged Johnny out the door.

Ringo stood with his back against the wall. This time, he

caught sight of my face before I could hide. He smirked and lifted a finger by his waist. The gun he'd formed with his hand clicked once, and he winked at me. Then the door shut him out.

"Is there a back way out of here?" I asked.

"Please?" Allie added to my question.

"Oh, in a hurry? You two crazy kids. You'll get the full treatment with the ceremony. That includes a limo ride straight to the airport or the *hotel* of your choice. You can skedaddle right out of the chapel through *my* entrance by the pulpit. It's all in your contract. Prepaid, *no* refunds." He skewered Allie with a raised eyebrow.

Allie blinked. "Who is going to officiate?" She glanced at me in Jerry's costume.

"I am. I can't have ol' Alfred Pulaski's granddaughter being hitched by some actor now, can I?"

Alfred…*Pulaski?* Son of a bitch.

Certain names are whispered in the circles I flirted with. Other names become legend. Allie's grandfather fit into the latter category. "How do we get this limo?"

"Sign right here. Print your full name under it." I did.

"And Ellie—"

"Allie."

The Justice paused for a second, "Right, Allie. I must have heard wrong. Please sign here. Print there. Good. All done. Meet me outside in five minutes. Go through that door and don't be late." He pointed at a back door I hadn't noticed.

"Oh, and Ellie, sorry, Allie, you might wanna put on your other wedding dress. That one's got a stain on it. Your parents are already logged into the live feed, just like you requested."

He chuckled as he snatched up the carbon copies of the paperwork we'd signed.

Allie groaned. "Shit. My parents were going to watch the show. I forgot about that."

4

ALLIE

Amore, Ti prometto di proteggerti con la mia vita. –
Love, I promise to protect you with my life

My parents didn't know the wedding was off. I shot a quick text off to Ellie. "You OWE me."

No reply. Damn it. She was probably passed out already.

"We have to wait five minutes." The Phantom paced the room, even peeked out the door Judge Stone went out of. "There are people out there."

"Guests?"

"You invited guests?" he asked. His tone rose in pitch slightly, and it didn't ruin his appeal. If I were the type of girl to swoon over sexy Italian men, he'd definitely do the trick. Especially ones with broad shoulders and a tight—

Before I got too sidetracked, I replied, "Ellie did."

I was surprised to discover my sister planned this wedding without me. She made sure the livestream of the ceremony went out to the whole family. Unfortunately, our parents couldn't leave the farm because the alpacas were expecting, and my father's parents didn't want to fly to Las Vegas because it had been thrown together at the last possible minute. But Grandpa Alfie's third mistress was out there with her whole country club ladies' mob and their escorts. Not husbands, the real deal, *escorts*. Worse? The reality TV show film crew who followed those women around had to be lurking in the corners. They never went anywhere without them.

And because of Ellie's surprisingly meticulous planning, calling off the wedding would create a shitstorm of questions and unregulated emotional outbursts. One I did not want to face alone. "I'm screwed."

"Why?"

He pressed on his ribcage with his right hand. He'd been favoring his left side since he wrestled with Johnny. "Because my mom and my dad's sister are absolutely enthralled with opera." I sighed. "And it's Vegas. It's all about the show." If I didn't at least *try* to go through with this ceremony, it was likely that one of the men in attendance would start his impersonation of *Magic Mike*. That alone would insure this fiasco made it to social media viral notoriety in minutes.

"Somehow that doesn't answer my question."

He had a rich voice, sexy accent, and damn him, a strong chin. His facial hair was gorgeously thick, but not overpowering. He wasn't neatly groomed, but not quite unruly. It was as if he'd spent a few days on the run and the beard had filled in where it would. It wandered up his strong jawline to brush against, but not fully connect to his expertly cut sideburns and sexy tapered haircut. The longer top perfectly suited a cluster of dark curls that fell forward but didn't obscure his thick eyebrows or those piercing brown eyes.

By Ellie's scale, he was an eleven. Maybe a twelve. In mine? Heck. I didn't have a scale. But if I did, he'd pass muster.

Or to be more truthful, create the high-water mark I'd forever judge everyone else by.

"Opera?" he prompted.

"Right. Ellie chose the Phantom of the Opera-themed event. A single red rose, the mask, this dress." I shook the clear bag containing Ellie's flowery dress of shame. Virginal and slutty all at once.

He studied the dress, then me. "It will look beautiful on you." He sounded sincere.

I huffed out an exasperated sigh. "I'm so screwed."

"How? We go out there, pretend to get married, and then leave. Explain later."

"We couldn't. That's against the rules, isn't it?" Or at least, it would be a hefty bending of them.

The phantom studied me. His lips were slightly canted as if he were considering some rule breaking. But only *slightly*. That sent a shiver snaking from my nipples to my—

A knock sounded on the door. A man asked, "Is everything okay in there?"

"Just fine!" Did I sound nervous? I wasn't nervous.

"You sure?"

I marched to the door and spoke very clearly to whoever it was. "Listen, we're just putting on some finishing touches.

We'll start in four minutes." Then I slumped against the door. "Kill me now."

Four minutes to get into that monstrosity and convince this stranger to play along. At least he was halfway there already. I turned and girded my argument with cold facts. "Okay. Bend the rules here a little, Allie." I stared him in the eyes. "We don't know each other, but here's how it's going to go. We walk down that aisle. Pretend we're *super* happy and everything is just fucking ducky. Kiss...*once*, and skedaddle right out of that back door we were promised. I'll tell the limo driver to drop you off anywhere you want. All you need to do is play along. Got it?"

"Excuse me?"

I narrowed my gaze on him. He was going to run. Then I'd have to face down Mom, Dad, Aunt Susan, the alpacas, and Vegas's answer to the Housewives of New Jersey, the film crew, and all those male strippers. "Consider your involvement an apology for stealing my ride earlier."

"I need to be at the airport."

"Great. That's where I'm going next. Is this a go?" Hopefully, I could straighten out the mess of my ticket being under Johnny's name. And, crossed fingers, I'd find someone there tonight rather than have to leave *extra* early in the morning to get things switched over. Because there was no way I was going to be able to convince Ellie to leave the hotel at oh-dark-thirty.

I searched his eyes.

He glanced to the main door, then the chapel entry. "Yes."

Hot dawg! I scrambled to unzip the bag and tug out the layers of tulle and ruffles. "I have to change. Turn around."

A softer knock on the door interrupted me, and the wedding planner slipped in. "We're ready?" She nodded hopefully.

"Except for the dress, can you help?" I asked.

She looked at the Phantom.

"Don't mind me, I'll just watch the wall for a few minutes."

"Cool. Ellie, are you okay with the groom being in here?"

"Absolutely. Let's do this thing." He'd turned his back like a gentleman, and the dress I currently wore was almost see-through, so I wasn't feeling any more embarrassed than if he'd seen me naked anyway.

The planner gushed as she prepped the gown. "Oh, thank you so much! It isn't every day we get a court officiator here, and I'd like to keep our business license, if you know what I mean?"

"You have nothing to worry about," The Phantom told the wall.

"Is Johnny going to be okay?" I asked as she fluffed the dress.

"I'm really sorry about letting him in. I didn't know he was your ex. They took him to Valley Hospital. I think he has a concussion. How hard did you hit him?" She gathered the dress into a bundled circlet of lace and tulle to drop over my head as she multi-tasked with her question.

The pause went a little too long.

Whoops, she was asking me. "Not nearly hard enough." My voice was muffled under the layers.

The Phantom snickered. Bloodthirsty bastard.

"Turn." I did as ordered, and the planner expertly zipped and tucked me into the gown.

Funny, I always thought I was thinner than Ellie. But *dear Lord* this dress was tight. My boobs were squished upward, and the large gap I'd thought was just a slit to flash skin actually had a fine flesh-toned mesh that held everything together and still managed to show off some impressive cleavage. I had cleavage!

With a quick twist and some clever bobby pin use, the planner had my hair knotted into an incredible waterfall of a messy updo that complemented the gown. "We don't have time for makeup, I'm sorry."

"Don't be, I don't like a lot of makeup." I ran a hand down the bodice. The delicate lace of the dropped shoulder draped loosely over my upper arms, and I looked like I'd stepped out of a fairy tale, or in this case, a Phantom's lair.

"Hey, Phantom, turn around."

My strange bridegroom turned to face me, and his jaw dropped a little. "Molta Bella," he whispered. His eyes dipped down the flesh-toned slash between my boobs and back up again to linger on my face. A series of words I didn't catch spilled from his lips like a benediction.

"You hear that? That's good." The wedding planner nudged me and fanned herself. "Ready?"

A wave of anxiety hit me. What if my parents didn't enjoy the show? It was supposed to be the Phantom marrying Ellie and Johnny, not me and… "Put on the mask."

My Phantom did as requested, the white half mask casting his face into shadows and mysterious angles. My heart beat triple time because this act seemed all too real. Hopefully, he wouldn't flub his lines.

But I really should have worried about my performance.

I shook in place as the soprano belted out one of the signature songs. My knees sent me all sorts of wobbly warning signs they were going to give out. Finally, it was time to say the vows.

"Do you, Mario Valentini, take this woman to be your lawfully wedded wife…"

Mario Valentini? I glanced up at my phantom to see if that was truly his name. He read my face and nodded once before saying, "I do."

Then it was my turn.

I shifted weight and almost went down. Mario caught my hand and let me lean on his strength. I squeezed hard.

"Do you, Allie Marie Jacobs, take this man to be your lawfully wedded husband, to have and to hold from this day forward, for better, for worse, for richer, for poorer, in sickness and in health, to love and to cherish, until parted by death. If so, please respond by saying, 'I do.'"

"I…" Oh shit this was *too* real. I glanced at the laptop someone propped up on a seat in the front row where my parents watched from their farm. They'd be so disappointed if I chickened out now. "I do."

The officiate smiled, and his voice boomed louder. "With the power invested in me by the people of Clark

County, Nevada, I now pronounce you husband and wife! Kiss her, you lucky dog."

Sell it, Allie.

Mario lifted his mask away, holding it between the audience and our little party of two plus the official. He made eye contact with me. Right before he leaned in, he checked the audience. A man in the third row whistled, then cupped his hands over his mouth, "Do it, Valentine. I dare you!"

With an apology written on his face, Mario pulled me close. "Amore, Ti prometto di proteggerti con la mia vita."

Whatever he said, it sounded perfect. I smiled as he drew closer. The whisper-soft brush of his lips made my eyes flutter shut, and I held on to his jacket so I wouldn't melt into a puddle. His lips were perfection. Full, lush, supple, yet strong, and I lost the script, kissing him like there was no tomorrow and we had moments left to live.

I was breathless when he broke the kiss to stare at me in wonder. My face must have reflected the same thing because, he'd stolen my soul with that kiss. "Wow," I breathed.

The audience broke out in laughter and then applause. I hid my face against Mario's chest as the embarrassment set in.

With trepidation, I checked the laptop where my parents hugged each other. I swore I could hear them say, "We love you, Ellie."

Not Allie.

That firmed my resolve. "Let's get out of here," I told Mario.

"With haste."

We almost broke into a full sprint to the limo that waited outside. The wedding planner was all smiles as she yelled, "Your things are in the car, arranged just like you requested, Congratulations!"

Not that the word was necessary. We'd done it. We'd fooled the entire crowd and given them a good show.

Mario checked behind us to see if anyone followed us out. I glanced back in time to see a man rush out of the entrance of the complex and race toward our chapel exit. He faded into the distance as the limo picked up speed.

"Where to?" The driver asked.

"Atlantic Aviation, I have a plane waiting," Mario directed.

I stared at him, taking in his profile, knowing I'd never truly have a man as handsome as he was for real. "It's been fun, hasn't it?"

He stared ahead, a bit lost in thought. Finally, he turned to me. "Come with me."

In my biggest fantasies, there was always a little bit of reality grounding me. I'd never dared to hope for someone to say to me something as impulsive as this. I barely knew him, and had only just learned his name. It was a ridiculous, but tempting proposition to say fuck it to everything. My crumbled career, the therapy sessions currently rehashing my control issues, the legal challenges that followed Grandfather's estate, the aftermath of Ellie's relationship implosion, and most of all, facing my parents and telling them it was all an act to bail Ellie out, again. Just once, I wanted to be the irresponsible sister and leave all the trouble behind rather than face it head-on and shoulder everyone else's burdens. I wanted to *live* the fantasy. That part asked, "Where are you going?"

"Italy."

Wasn't that convenient? "I'm going there, too."

"Yes, with me, should you want to."

I laughed. He sounded so certain. "No, I'm supposed to meet my sister at the hotel. But I need to go to the airport to switch Johnny's ticket to mine, then we'll leave at 11 AM to fly to Denver, then from there to Venice."

Mario stared at me with those soft, but intense eyes. "You won't have to switch the ticket. We'll get there faster in my jet."

My heart beat a little faster. Not only was he a fantasy in the flesh, but for him to be rich was right out of la-la land. I wasn't a sucker…yet. "You own a jet?"

"It's the company's, but in part, yes."

That sounded more plausible.

And crazy. He was so far out of my league. "What about Ellie?"

"She has a ticket, no? You'll meet her there. Please?"

My heart wanted to jump out of my chest. This was huge. "Are you serious?"

"To a fault. I mean, surprisingly I am…yes."

He sounded sincere. I wanted to open my mouth and grill him for details. Logistics. Plans. But underneath all that noise was a voice. Ellie's. *Live a little.* "You're not going to kill me, are you?"

"Absolutely not. That would be against the code."

A code was much better than false promises. Of course,

sometimes it was worse if you ran afoul of it. Was this the good kind or the bad kind? "You have a code?"

He nodded solemnly. "Yes. And upon that code, I *vow* you will be safe, Allie Jacobs." His face shifted. "Probably safer than with your sister."

I laughed, slightly relieved, and because he was right. "That's the truth. So…Italy? Do you think I'll beat her there?" Sue me. We'd been in competition since birth. Likely before.

"Absolutemente."

Ding! Extra bonus, he knew the language and his accent was real. Not mangled like mine due to the online language courses I'd been taking over the years. "Are you from there?"

"My father is, so, yes."

"Where do you live?" The real Allie was peeking out with her twenty-question quota.

"Here, there."

That wasn't an answer, and a tiny warning light flashed in my brain. "That's not specific, where?"

"Mostly Liguria and Sardinia. New York when I have business there. Milan, Los Angeles, Miami, London…"

I refrained from asking something uncouth like, 'How much money do you have?' That would be countered with how much money do *you* have? Which right now could be summed up with, "None I wanted to touch."

And I really couldn't answer the questions that statement would trigger. Grandfather's trust gave me an allowance that was generous, but I refused to do what Ellie did and spend it willy-nilly as soon as it hit my fingertips. I was saving. For what, I didn't know. Hopefully, a small farm, a private practice, some place where no one knew who my grandfather was, or at least didn't care if he'd been the mob's accountant. And hopefully in a secure enough location that a sudden catastrophe wouldn't would rip that private and peaceful life away from me. Maybe I couldn't accept the money was real because I knew there was no escape from the source of it.

The limo pulled into the private airlines' terminal. Mario got out with the driver and sent him into the terminal to arrange the flight. Then Mario paced around the car. If I were Ellie, I'd be taking notes about the sculptural perfection of his ass. But I refrained, instead texting on my phone.

"El, I have to do something. I'm sorry. I WILL meet you in Venice. Cash in the extra ticket."

A second later, my phone buzzed with a text from Ellie.

"You BETTER meet me there, or I'm calling Mom."

I shot back a reply,

"I will. Slight detour. Will you be okay by yourself?"
"Aren't I always? Don't strain yourself by worrying about me."

I texted back another apology, but she didn't reply. Her usual M.O. when I'd pissed her off. I tucked the phone back into my tote bag. Was I truly considering this?

Yes. I meant it when I told my sister I had to do this. I'd regret it if I didn't, and I was tired of regretting things. I sent Mario a nod and a thumbs up through the window.

Then, I took inventory. My bridesmaid's dress was zippered up in a bag provided by the venue. It draped across the seat opposite me. Did I have any other clothing? I didn't want to put that back on.

"Oh shit," I muttered and frantically dug in the tote I'd packed for the wedding center. *Double shit.* I hadn't planned for more than essential items to help Ellie, and a comfortable change of clothing for me once the ceremony was complete. Ellie's bag was bound to be much worse. Maybe I'd luck out, and she packed dresses in the lonely carry-on in the trunk.

"Is everything okay?" Mario leaned in the open door.

"I have one change of clothes, and whatever Ellie packed, if you don't count these." I motioned to myself and the dress in the bag.

He smiled and slipped into the seat next to me. "We'll fix that. In eleven hours or so, we'll land in the fashion capital of the world. I'm sure you'll find everything you need." He tried to return his face to the stoic mask he'd had on when talking to the driver, but his cheek quirked into a little dimple.

Mario Valentini had a dimple. I fought the urge to fan myself.

The driver returned and pulled the car around to the back of the building. He parked beside a rather large plane that had the passenger stairs readied for boarding. The driver opened the door for us, and stewards from the flight company took my bags to a loading hatch at the back of the plane. "I need that tote—"

Mario steered me toward the stairs connecting to the front.

"I need my bag."

"Don't worry. You'll have access to it."

I wanted to protest, but there were people ushering us onto the jet and fussing over the preparations to depart. A man from the airline staff stood at the top of the stairs.

"Mr. Valentini, the pilots are ready. The plane is prepared. You have a crew of five, and your things are in the stateroom storage. Edward sends his regards." He noticed me, the dress I wore, and added, "And this beautiful woman is?"

"My wife."

The attendant's mouth opened and shut. "I see. Congratulations." With that, he stepped to the side of the jet stairs, and allowed us to enter.

"I'm not your wife," I whispered to Mario, then smiled at a female attendant who led us to a grouping of four seats. Beyond them was a table with seating room for four comfortably. A third section filled the back of the cabin, which had a couch and another set of two chairs facing each other. "Where's my bag?" I scanned the seats for signs of it.

"This way, Mrs. Valentini."

At her honorific, I shot a glare at Mario. He smiled slyly and stepped aside so the stewardess could lead me to the back. Beyond the last section with the couch and two chairs was a door leading to the largest airplane bathroom I'd ever seen. It came complete with a little window next to the sink that had its own makeup mirror to the left, and through one more sliding door, my things were piled neatly on shelves, and the bridesmaid dress and the empty bag for the dress I was wearing were hanging in a small closet. There were two suits hung there as well. I fingered them one at a time. One was silk and the other, a very fine wool. Nice.

The stewardess opened a couple of drawers in the bathroom showing me where extra toothbrushes and all the accompanying necessaries were. "I hope you enjoy your flight, did you want coffee, wine… champagne?"

What the hell. While I was being impulsive, I might as well milk this for all it was worth, because when the bubble burst, I'd regret not taking full advantage of the situation. "Champagne."

"Excellent choice." She dipped her head and left me alone to marvel at the incredibly useful and yet brazenly opulent space.

"I've died and gone to heaven." That was the only explanation for all of this.

"Allie?" Mario broke into my reverie with a light knock on the open door to the bathroom. "We need to depart. The tower has cleared the flight."

"I'm going to Italy." In style.

5

MARIO

I gritted my teeth as each small imperfection in the runway jarred through the wheels, up the structure of the plane, and into my ribs. The seat's belt dug into the pressure bandage I'd applied.

Allie stared out the window at the city we escaped. "I hope Ellie makes her flight."

"Is your sister impaired?" The pain made me less than eloquent.

Allie huffed out a laugh. "No, I just worry is all."

Ah. I knew that temptation. Without me, Ringo would be lost. *Good*.

And right as the wheels lifted into the air, an especially hard jolt raked the bandage across my wound and I wished him all the ill travels possible. Then the acceleration pressed me back against the seat, and I had to forget about anything but trying not to voice the pain out loud. I closed my eyes and gritted my teeth to bear it.

Once the jet leveled off, Allie disappeared into the back. She reemerged dressed in a pale honey-colored cotton T-shirt and lightweight dark pants that hugged her subtle curves. Her hair was still up, but in a sedate ponytail rather than the half-fallen updo the planner had created. This was the real woman peeking out. She was pleasing to the eye. Allie had long legs, a narrow waist, and an athletic build.

The wedding dress she wore earlier gave the illusion she was much more well-endowed on top than the reality.

But I liked the real her much better than fantasy.

She wasn't wearing a bra.

I tried not to stare.

"I now pronounce you husband and wife."

I'd kept our copy of the paperwork we signed at the wedding center. In plain language, we'd been duped by the Justice of the Peace. He'd made it sound like we were signing the venue contract for the limousine service. In reality, it was a marriage license…a very *legal* marriage license.

I couldn't marry Dianora now. With that mistake, I was destined to die much sooner than I planned.

Somehow, that didn't register emotionally. Yes, of course I was disappointed I no longer had an easy option to stay alive, but unlike most, I thrived when challenged. This was more than that, however. It was a battle for my life. Anticipation would be closer to an accurate way to describe what I was feeling. I had a challenge and a beautiful wife. One who presented as amenable, kind… soft.

Those thoughts weren't appropriate. Perhaps I was tired.

It was well after midnight. Flying eastward, we'd cross…was it six or seven time zones? My brain was foggy with pain.

"I must be tired."

Allie heard my complaint and leaned across the aisle. She placed a hand on mine. "Are you okay?"

No. My wound throbbed, was warm, and the blood loss was making me weak. The plans I'd made to survive were in tatters. And my best friend not only stabbed me, but watched me flush my life down the toilet by marrying the wrong woman, and he didn't say one word.

Wait. He did speak. He *dared* me to sabotage myself. *Idiot.* He'd signed his own death warrant, too. Unless he succeeded in killing me.

Instead of answering her, I handed the paper to Allie. "Read this, please?"

Her brows furrowed for a moment, but she took the page from my hand. Her hands were narrowly delicate in build, but not pampered. I longed to trace my fingers down the length of each finger to discover their nuances.

She read in silence for all of a minute. Then, returned her attention to the top of the page where it clearly stated the intent of the contract.

"This can't be right."

Nothing had gone correctly in a week. At this point, I was immune to the shock. Allie, however was not.

"We're married?"

"Say it louder so the staff can hear your disgust." I shot her a warning with my eyes. But the staff were already whispering.

A range of emotions flickered across her face. Defiance,

anger, fright, and then something cautious settled into the line of her tight lips.

"We can get it annulled," she said softly.

We could. But I'd had at least ten minutes or more to create contingency plans. And once those took shape, I figured I could use this complication to my advantage. "We could. If we were in Las Vegas. Here, we can't. And when we land it will not be easy."

The stewardess brought Allie a glass of champagne. Its mate was on the tray she balanced.

I waved her off. "Water."

As the stewardess retreated, Allie frowned and stared at her glass. "I don't feel like celebrating now." She set the glass on the ledge near the window.

There was a little table hidden in a pocket under where she set the glass. I pressed the latch for mine and pulled it out, being certain she watched how it was done. She picked up the glass, sipped off a small portion and then mimicked my motions. Once her glass was on safer ground, and the cabin staff returned to the front of the plane, I leaned back to press my palm over the worst of the pain. She probably hated me for tempting her along on this trip.

"What's wrong?"

"It's nothing," I lied.

She studied me, taking one more sip before grimacing and setting the glass down again. "You wouldn't know this, but I used to volunteer for a mobile veterinary service in northern Illinois. One of the farms had an old dog named Charlie. He hid a limp from his owner so well, his regular vet didn't even notice it. But I was new and saw the way

Charlie couldn't walk in a straight line. He'd compensate for it by taking two steps sideways before moving. His owner thought it was just something the dog did because he was getting old."

I set my hand on my knee, determined not to show any more weakness.

Her eyes followed the motion. The frown on her face tightened.

"After finishing with the horse I'd been called out for, I asked if I could pet Charlie. The man warned me he bit folks who'd get too close." Her expression twisted into a question, but it didn't beg for an answer.

I speculated instead. "Let me guess, the dog was in pain."

"That's right."

She let the silence fill the air around us. I should use it to admit my secret. But I didn't.

Once she'd let enough time pass, she continued. "I took my time. He had a broken rib that was almost healed, but that poor thing had suffered so long, he…" she trailed off, obviously broken-hearted over the poor animal's pain.

Was I wrong about her? "How'd you get Charlie to trust you?"

The corner of her mouth went up. Then she picked up her glass and slipped out of her seat to kneel on the floor between us. "I sat like this and waited for him to approach."

This close, I caught the scent of the perfume she wore. I'd captured notes of it before. The first time was when I bumped into her before I stole her ride. It distracted me then, now it tempted me to touch her.

"That's all?"

A shoulder went up. "Animals can't talk, and despite what some people think, they don't really understand words. However, they *do* understand body language. I showed Charlie I'm not a threat. That's how I was able to help him."

She took a sip of her champagne. Her eyes darted to mine.

I motioned for her to hand me her glass. The tart flavor burst on my tongue.

There was over half of the glass remaining. I passed it back to her. And opened my water.

She stared at it for a moment and lifted it slightly. "Here's to our marriage?"

Her throat was fascinating to watch as she swallowed. She stared at the carpet for a moment, then looked up at me and smiled.

The glass in her hand was offered gently. Instead of forcing it into my space, she held it within hers.

That old dog hadn't had a chance against her wiles. I unbuckled and shifted forward so I wouldn't have to bend against my wound as I took the glass from her hand. "*To my beautiful and smart wife. May she always think of me kindly, even if I don't deserve it.*"

She wouldn't understand my toast because I spoke in my grandfather's tongue. He was born in Gallura on Sardinia. The dialect he'd been born to was spoken centuries before the modern Italian.

I only used it around him and the immediate family there. Or, if I needed to keep my own secrets.

When I completed my toast, I emptied the glass. The stewardess offered a refill, but I refused. "We're ready to retire. Please?" I motioned for her to prepare the back suite.

She did as asked.

Allie leaned a bit to observe the activity at the back of the cabin. "One bed…"

I took that moment to brush her cheek.

Trust went both ways.

"I won't pressure you." Not that I would. Nor could in my condition.

Her lips parted as my fingers paused at her jawline.

This time, I did lean in, ignoring the sharp bite of pain. Her eyes were a mixed canvas of green and brown and blue. There was no reason to it, just chaos that started as a pale earthy green then spread into a kaleidoscope of colors before the deeply-colored edges shifted from almost brown to deep blue in the light.

I wanted to kiss her again. My carnal desires for her tempted me to turn against my code and just take her for my own.

"The suite is ready."

I acknowledged the stewardess's interruption. Carefully, I stood and offered Allie a hand to help her stand.

She put her hand in mine, but stood without putting weight on me by using her free arm for leverage. Even without speaking, I'd given my secrets away.

It was a relief to slide the bulkhead privacy door closed. My shoulders dipped as the stress of the day lessened. For the moment, I was as safe as I could be.

"Let's see where you're hurt."

I looked over my shoulder at Allie.

She motioned to my side.

"It is nothing."

Instead of arguing with me, she went through the lavatory to the luggage storage behind it. When she returned, she carried a garment bag. It wasn't the clear one with the wedding dress in it.

It was the *other* dress. The one that made her appear naked. Despite the fatigue and the wound, my cock hardened from the memory of her in it.

She unzipped the bag and tugged out enough fabric to reveal a rust-colored stain on it. "That's your blood, I believe?"

I swallowed.

"It was on my hands." Her voice was hard. She quickly stuffed the dress back into its bag and tossed it over one seat. "Sit down."

Allie pointed to the turned-down duvet, now spread across a bed big enough to fit both of us.

Reluctantly, I followed her orders.

She tugged at her T-shirt, indicating I should unbutton my shirt.

"A mobile veterinary service?"

"I'm a licensed veterinary surgeon. At least they couldn't take *that* from me." The latter half was muttered to herself. Amusing, and a puzzle to solve…later. I unbuttoned my shirt and removed it so she could get a good look at the mess I'd made of myself.

Other than a subtle shift of her eyes as she scanned my chest and dipped lower, she kept her composure. "When did someone field dress this?"

She hadn't approached. I was still that old dog who'd bite.

"I did this about ten to fifteen minutes before the wedding."

Allie nodded to herself. "Not in the car, right?"

"No." That would be stupid.

I spilled out at least one of my secrets and told her about the tattoo parlor.

She took a step forward and stopped. "May I?"

"I promise not to bite…hard." What was I doing? Flirting? That wasn't me. I must be addled.

Allie placed the back of her hand on my neck. "You're warm. That's not good."

Her ministrations moved lower, and I sucked in a breath when she touched the tender skin above the wound.

"Normally, I'd say leave the dressing on until we get to a hospital, but…"

"I can wait eleven hours."

Her eyes bored into mine. "You think so, huh?" The words challenged me.

"I know so."

That didn't get the reaction I'd intended. Her nimble fingers slipped the pad up while her other hand pressed me flat onto the bed.

"The bleeding has stopped. That's good. You should get stitches, though." The corners of her mouth tightened. "Does this hurt?" Her fingers pressed down on a spot about one inch from the wound.

I flinched.

"That's a yep." She shifted to inspect another section. This time her fingers were lighter as she prodded. Then she sat on the bed next to me. "You need antibiotics, stitches, and rest."

I slid a glance at the bed I was on.

She understood, but frowned. "I'm going to see if there is a first aid kit."

"No." I caught her hand before she could stand.

Allie slipped it out of my grip. "Listen, we can do this the easy way, or the hard way. But either way, I'm going to get you some pain reliever and a fresh bandage. This one is shit."

"Don't tell them I'm injured."

Her eyebrow shot up. "Why not?"

I debated how much I could trust her. Perhaps a small gamble wouldn't hurt? "What do you think caused my wound?" I knew the answer, but this was a test.

The narrowing of her eyes told me almost as much as I needed to know. "Quite possibly, a knife. Something sharp and angled like this when it entered here and glanced off here." Her hand followed the line of Ringo's thrust.

She already knew too much. But then she sealed her fate. "Did you know your liver extends from here up to here, and angles like this across your abdomen?" Her finger brushed my skin.

The liver being one of the major organs that, if damaged, could likely result in death. One not as long or as lingering as stabbing me in the small intestine, but a much more painful process than catching my lung would have been. Ringo aimed his strike with intention to make me regret every hour of my death with agony. I'd been lucky to catch his hand and deflect it.

Allie stared at the wound site she'd lightly covered. "I'll tell them I have an allergy and that I would feel better if it were at hand. Okay?"

Instead of letting her leave me, I leaned to activate the communication service. "Please send the stewardess to the back with the first aid kit. My wife has a headache."

Allie rolled her eyes.

I shifted the sheet, so it covered my stomach and the bandages.

To my surprise, Allie tugged off her pants, exposing her long legs. The stewardess knocked on the panel before opening the sliding door. Her gaze dipped from Allie's state of undress to mine on the bed. With as much professionalism she could muster, she handed off the case without comment and slid the panel shut giving us privacy again.

"You didn't have to do that."

Allie shrugged. "Better than getting blood on my pants. Do you know how hard that is to get out?"

I doubted she knew exactly how difficult some blood stains were to remove.

Then again, she was a surgeon who dealt with animals. Her quick work to rummage through the kit, moving some items to the side and repacking others made me rethink her expertise. Notably, she kept out three things that concerned me. Foremost were the epinephrin and the atropine. The first would be helpful if my heart stopped, and the second effective if it didn't start up again.

"We won't need those."

Her glare dared me to shut up. "Just in case."

If I died, I wanted neither. "Allie."

She rummaged harder, searching each closed pouch and box.

"There's *nothing* in here for stitches, and it's worthless for deep sterilization. Even if I could strip some of the silk from that damn wedding dress, this case is fucking useless. Here." She handed me two over-the-counter pain pills. I swallowed them with a sip from the water bottle I'd brought back with us.

"Your bedside manner could use some work."

"Animals don't give a shit about manners."

Despite myself, I laughed. Then tried to take my pants and shoes off.

But the pain was humbling.

"Let me." Allie tugged off my shoes, undid my belt, and worked each pant leg off gently.

By the time I was down to my boxers, a fine sweat covered my skin. I shivered.

"That's it. Get under the sheets."

I thought you'd never ask.

Funny how that sounded like Ringo in my head.

Belatedly, I realized I hadn't made room for Allie. I shifted closer to the windows.

"Don't. These chairs recline, right?"

I nodded.

"Okay. Sleep. You need it."

I tried, I really did, but somewhere over the Atlantic, my

fever got worse. Allie checked on me and placed a cold washcloth on my head.

"Who did this to you?"

"It's better if you don't know."

She frowned and let me toss for another hour in agony.

Between the waves of heat and the thrumming fire tormenting my side, I had a momentary dream. Ringo slipped through the bulkhead dressed from head to toe in black.

"How'd you get in here?"

"Through the door, like everyone else." He smiled, then looked at Allie's sleeping form on the chair across from me. Ringo's grin grew wider. "Have you gotten a piece of that yet?"

"No."

He sighed. "Are you going to be a Boy Scout your entire life? Let me fix that for you." He slipped his knife out and sliced her throat.

I sat up straight in the bed and reached for her, but the aisle was miles wide. Her blood poured onto the carpet.

"No!"

I landed on the floor at Allie's feet. That jolted her awake. She rolled me over and quickly checked the bandages for damage. "Did you fall out of bed?"

Ringo was nowhere to be found. And Allie was whole.

My breaths were too frantic, and my skin was too warm. "He said he'd kill me, and he did."

"You're not going to die." She helped me get back into bed and straightened the sheets before retrieving another cold washcloth.

"Allie—"

"Nope, shush. I've got you."

But who would protect her? I tugged the ring on my pinky off. It was a simple token, one I should have given her earlier. "Put this on. The crest points away from your hand in this way so others know who you belong to. Do not forget."

Her forehead creased with concern.

I cut off her objections before she could voice them. "When we land, if I'm unconscious or unable to stay with you, you will speak for me, and with this ring positioned so, *as* me. Do you understand? You will show this ring to whoever you need to. Tell them—"

"No, here's what's going to happen. You'll take the medicine I'm giving you, sleep if you can, and by the time the fever and pain seem like it's too awful to survive, we'll be on the ground and go to the nearest hospital. I'll need to tell the flight—"

"No!"

"Mario, you need a hospital."

"I need a phone." Why hadn't I thought this through earlier?

Allie rummaged through her bag and tugged out her cellphone.

It couldn't be that simple, could it? "Does it have a signal?"

She checked it. "No." Her shoulders slumped.

I didn't expect it to. "There is a satellite phone in the conference area. It is secure. I will get—ow." A wave of dizziness knocked me onto my back.

"I'll go."

If there was a woman out there for me, Allie had ruined their chances, because she was everything I needed. "Do you have paper, a pen?"

Allie pulled the items from her bag. I jotted down my father's number. He'd be closest. And the most brutal, but I couldn't delay longer. "Ask for Signore Niccolò Valentini. Confirm the line is secure and that he understands you are calling on behalf of me. Tell him I asked for Zio Tommaso to meet us at the penthouse. When the call is complete, bring a bottle of wine and some food back here. Do not tell *anyone* I'm injured. Do not let anyone help you. Show them that ring if you have to."

"Don't you trust them?"

"I don't trust anyone." I couldn't anymore.

She glanced at the bandages. "I suppose you don't."

I caught her hand. "I am sorry."

Her hand fisted. Despite that, her tone was soft. "For what?"

Maybe it was time? "For not being a good husband."

A silent laugh shook her shoulders once. The smile it caused faded. "You're not going to die."

"Zio Tommaso. Understand?"

"Your uncle, he's a doctor?"

She understood me? "It is code."

"But not *the* code, right?"

I couched my words, hoping she'd understand the situation better. "Your grandfather?"

Her jaw worked sideways. "What about him?"

I closed my eyes, hoping I would be wrong. "He was an accountant, no?"

My peek at her was brief. She'd pinched her lips together so tightly, they turned white.

I continued. "His clients were…"

"Criminals," she supplied.

Damn it. "But you understand code and *the* code?" I let go of her hand.

She twisted at the ring I'd slipped on her left hand. "Is this your family crest?"

I nodded once.

Her face shifted as she stared at her finger. "You know, most mob wives get a honking diamond."

The sarcasm in her tone spoke louder than words. I brushed her hand with mine. "But their queens do not." I dropped my hand and gave her silent permission to ruin my life. What remained of it.

6

ALLIE

When Mario said we were landing in the fashion capital of the world, I thought he meant it figuratively, like the country or vicinity, not the fucking *city*.

Milan.

It was everything I'd imagined, and nothing like I'd dreamed. Except maybe in nightmares. We'd left in darkness and landed in darkness. It threw me off completely. An entire day crossed over and measured in fever checks and lies.

The skyline zipped by in smears of neon and incandescent lights as a bruiser of a man named Loppa drove us to a charming period building within walking distance of the town center and tucked into a residential neighborhood so palatial, it might as well have armed gates at the end of each block.

As I helped Mario from the car, Loppa snatched him away without a word. The excuse we gave the flight crew for

Mario's imbalance was that he was drunk. The two bottles of wine I'd snagged from the custom wine cabinet at the front of the plane were the supposed culprit for his inability to walk without assistance. In reality, his fever was so high, I was afraid he'd fall down the stairs without someone to hold him upright.

We hadn't drank a drop of the expensive liquid.

And I kept up the facade of "happy wife." Although, deep inside I fumed at every delay, question, or judgmental inspection.

When we finally exited a severely slow elevator, I directed Loppa to deposit Mario on the deep blue, artistic sofa directly inside. "Where is this Zio Tommaso?" I asked.

A distinguished man stepped into the lit room. His hair was completely gray, but he carried himself with such poise and authority, I immediately changed my tone. "Hello, are you Zi—"

He held up a hand. In rapid-fire Italian he addressed Mario.

My…husband replied in weary tones. His face was pale despite his natural coloring. I sat down beside him to hold his hand, and potentially catch him should he fall over. That became more likely as the questions wore on.

Loppa discreetly studied the terrace and the city skyline while Mario drooped further.

Finally, Mario said something in English that I understood. "This is Allie, my wife."

The bastard interrogating him said something crude, or at least his tone inferred it. I studied Mario's expression to gauge whether I should be insulted or not.

There was a big wall of nothing there. It was so emotionless, it held a power of its very own. He closed his eyes briefly as the man wound down his tirade. "Allie, this is my father. You spoke with him on the phone."

Ah, yes, the *asshole*.

I wouldn't shake his hand, that's for sure. "Did you call a doctor?"

Something flickered across his face, but like his son, he had his emotions locked down tight. He directed Loppa to do something. The man disappeared, then returned with a stooped little man carrying a black bag.

When he opened that bag, I'd ascertained this was "Zio Tommaso." But Loppa called him by his honorific, Dottor.

He began his examination of Mario and I hovered with more than a professional curiosity. Maybe my new husband's paranoia had rubbed off onto me, but I scrutinized the doctor's actions.

When he injected Mario with something, I almost snatched it out of his hand. Instead, I counted to three before picking up the vial and reading the label. Thank goodness for all the Latin I'd taken in my post-graduate study.

It was an antibiotic. One that was extremely effective in surgical settings. He brought out a bottle of pills and directed both Mario and me on the dosage over the next five days. Then he handed Mario two pills while I inspected the label.

It was a fairly potent pain medicine.

Then he applied a topical so he could irrigate the wound

and remove a bit of fabric from the deepest section. I acted as the surgical nurse for the worst of it.

His stitches were much more precise than mine would have been. The wound, despite the swelling, was much less life-threatening now. I breathed a small sigh of relief.

"He'll live." The doctor declared. Mostly to me because he spoke in English. To the others, there was a longer explanation, but effectively the same diagnosis.

I thanked the man with a nod before Mario's father led him away.

Mario still leaned on the cushions, not bothering to button his shirt, or do much more than breathe. I checked his forehead for any break in the fever. There was none. But his color was better.

"Is there a place to rest?" I wasn't sure Loppa knew English or not, but asked anyway.

But the reply came from Mario's father who'd returned a little too quickly. "You will sleep in the maid's quarters. Mario will take the—"

"We're sleeping together," Mario declared to his father. He placed a possessive hand high on my thigh.

I covered it with my own because I was too invested in his well-being to just walk away.

His father glanced down at the ring on my finger. It lingered, sifting through the significance of it with meticulous animosity. Cold eyes met mine. "How long have you known my son?"

I wasn't going to lie, nor was I going to tell the truth. "Long enough to know he won't be safe here if I left him."

Loppa snorted, outing himself. He did understand me despite the way he'd silently ignored me since the airport.

The answer wasn't met with as much amusement on his father's part. "You are an American." He scrunched his nose as if he were trying to block out something rancid.

That didn't deserve a reply, because…*duh.*

He left us with a curt, "I'll take my leave," instead of saying "good night."

Loppa suggested something.

"I wish he'd speak English," I muttered. My brief exposure through an online app would not cut it in this country.

Mario translated. "He said I'd rest easier at the villa. And I would, but it is too far to travel tonight." He directed his next sentence to Loppa. "And that's the first place he'd look for me. This"—Mario motioned with his hand to encompass the posh penthouse suite—"would be the very last place he'd *want* to find me at."

"Bastardo," Loppa muttered.

I knew that word. "Who's the bastard? The guy who stabbed you?"

Mario closed his eyes, the pain or exhaustion making it difficult for him to answer me while looking at me directly. "My best friend, Ringo."

I blinked.

In my mind's eye, I saw the man who'd ran up to me after Mario stole my ride share. And he'd seen me and Ellie. *I saw you two at the casino.* Come to think of it, I might have noticed Ringo with Mario when I rushed into the lobby to find my sister. They'd seemed chummy enough at the time.

And I hadn't given it much thought, but somewhere in my brain, I put the pieces of the scene together along with the blood on my hand. He was even at the ceremony and followed us out as we fled. Luckily, he hadn't caught us. "Why would your best friend do that?"

"Twelve million American dollars," Loppa stated plainly.

"Seven," Mario whispered.

"No, it is twelve now. You are an expensive trophy." He was having too much fun correcting Mario. And while this was way beyond my safe zone, it didn't surprise me one bit. I'd had more than enough time to fret on the organized crime angle of it all while watching Mario attempt to sleep.

He knew exactly who my grandfather was.

Before we got married.

And did it anyway. *Who was the bastard here?* Because only Loppa showed any kind of honor.

I should have stuck to my plan to fly with Ellie. I could have walked away then with the limo driver as witness. Normally, I would have. It would have been the smart thing to do. Unless…

Was Mario the kind of man who'd have someone killed if they deviated from his plans?

His father sure was. That polished veneer was too calculating for comfort. "What does your father do?"

Mario opened an eye to figure out my subject change. "He is the head of the trade organization."

"That's a thing?" Maybe if I paid more attention to my grandfather's profession when he was alive, I'd know that.

"Sì." Mario was fading a little too quickly.

Loppa corrected my assumptions. "Don Valentini is Italy's trade minister."

It took me a moment to put it together. "He's a politician?" On the evil authority figure scale, they had to be the worst.

"It's not obvious?" Mario gritted through his teeth as he shifted upright.

The dental veneers should have tipped me off. Or the cold, almost sterile, white on white marble of his home. I took the moment to scan the room. Two foot wide white marble columns braced the arching white ceiling. The moonlight-pale marble under my feet stretched from wall to wall. Sure, there were splashes of bright color, like the sofa. But it was all strategically placed and entirely devoid of emotion. A showplace for entertaining and impressing, but not a home. Even Grandfather hadn't been that cold. "Bastardo."

Mario snorted. "Don't let him hear you say that."

"Or what? He'll have me deported, arrested?" Stalked? I shuddered.

"He could," Loppa supplied helpfully.

Mario sighed and slumped off-kilter to favor his side. "Then I'd go with her." The weariness and painkillers were doing him in.

"Your grandfather would be angry if you left too quickly. He'll want to meet this woman you call your wife."

Mario lifted his head to study Loppa. "When I am feeling better, maybe tomorrow, we'll go there. Not even the master of assassins would be stupid enough to kill me on Don Manca's soil."

Loppa didn't reply. And notably, he didn't smile at the idea of traveling somewhere else.

A thought struck me as we sat in silence. "This friend of yours, he's not the master of assassins, is he?" Was there such a thing?

Mario was slow to answer. "He'd like to think so. But even he isn't that good." He motioned to Loppa to help him stand.

Did that imply there was *a master of assassins?*

Loppa held Mario as he climbed the stairs to our room. In the crystal clear starlight, the city looked beautiful, but also sinister. I paced while Loppa helped my husband get comfortable as he succumbed to the pain medicine. *I have a husband.*

"Signora?"

Loppa's soft question got my attention. "Yes?"

He glanced at the bed. "I noticed blood doesn't bother you. Correct?"

I nodded. Not blood, or much else. I'd seen so much worse on patients who couldn't even voice their fear or describe the pain they were in.

His hulking form joined me as I stared out at the rooftops and skyline in front of me. "That's good."

"This friend of his, he's not really an assassin, is he?"

Loppa glanced at Mario's sleeping form. He measured his words very carefully. "His friend is a nothing."

That was more cryptic than a flat-out denial.

I studied him. "Are you an assassin?"

"No."

"Interesting."

Loppa stepped backward suddenly aware of me as more than he'd estimated. "What is interesting?"

I smiled, trying to soften my words for his sake. "You quickly denied my question about you, but didn't deny the other question. Why is that?"

His eyes picked up the light from outside. Just a glint of reflection, then gone as his brows lowered. "Some people shouldn't be discussed casually."

Kind of like my grandfather.

An accountant, *my ass*. Or maybe, that was really who he was. But as one, he knew all of his clients' dirty little secrets. And *they* were the type of person who shouldn't be discussed casually.

Which was why I hadn't touched that money. Worry ate at me over my inheritance. What if there was someone out there who wanted that money? And what if that someone was ruthless enough to take it by whatever means necessary? Or what if they took it through duplicitous means, like marrying me? A chill tickled the edges of my back. I hugged myself to rub it away.

Maybe Ellie had the right idea. Spend it as soon as it hit the bank. That way it was gone, and then no one would get any funny ideas about taking it.

Then again, if someone took it from me, I'd no longer have it hanging over my head like a proverbial sword. Somehow, that was comforting. Mario could have the money if that was his motive for marrying me. Then again, I almost coerced him into it. Did he resent me for that? I didn't mean to trick him.

Was it only a day ago that we'd bumped into each other?

In total hours it was less than a day, but nearly two by dateline and time zones. The math escaped me in the moment. I stared at a smiling moon so similar to the one I'd seen shining over the Las Vegas skyline right after getting married.

And I still hadn't called my mother to tell her it wasn't a real wedding. *Ugh.*

"I need to be in Venice tomorrow," I told Loppa.

"You won't be in Venice." He sat in a chair that he'd shoved against the door.

I promised Ellie I'd be there. I told him as much.

"You won't be in Venice," he repeated. Then he tacked on, "You'll be right here because *he* needs you." His head tipped toward Mario.

Loppa might be strong, but he was also too damn smart. He'd already found my weakness and exploited it.

Bastardo.

7

MARIO

My father gave me one night of peace. But that was only because he was calculating the best way to ruin the plans I'd made. Though instructed to rest by a doctor, and one stubborn, but cute veterinarian, I needed to remain one step ahead of my enemies. And that included my father.

One of those steps was to provide Allie the armor she needed to disable the enemies she'd inherited from me.

"I can't wear this." She plucked at the shimmering pale gold sheath dress hugging every curve of her body.

The rejection rack was more crowded than the begrudgingly accepted one.

"It looks exceptional on you." I especially liked the deep slit that flashed her bare leg.

Her head tipped sarcastically at me. "If you'd just let me call my sister, I'd have my things and—"

The couture stilista didn't hide her thoughts on the

matter. A string of rapid-fire judgments about Allie's style flew from her lips. None of it registered on Allie, but they gouged deep in my heart.

Allie was not plain, nor provincial. She was classic, reserved, and strong of both mind and heart.

Despite orders from both my physician and a beautiful veterinarian, I stood. "Enough."

Everyone except Allie froze. She hurried to my side and hissed, "Sit down before you fall down." Her hand rested on my hip bone, just below the line of stitches.

Under my breath, I corrected her. "It doesn't hurt." To soften the rebuke, I pulled her hand to my lips. "Trust me."

Her nostrils flared, but she knew better than to argue with me in front of the small army who'd invaded our temporary home.

"It is obvious my wife prefers a more classic look. She has refined needs. Judging by the choices she's made, she prefers comfort, utility, and timelessness, not whimsy. Think royalty, not vulgarian."

With the fanfare of a carnival barker, the stylist brought in two more racks of clothing. The existing ones, save for the few core pieces Allie chose, were whisked away.

In the end, she chose an elegant, muted-sage dress. It was clean-lined with a hint of softness at the neckline where it draped artfully without exposing more than her collarbone. Her honey-blonde hair curled slightly over one shoulder and rested on her chest, daring me to touch.

I conveyed my approval with a nod and only a small tightening of my mouth toward a smile. I longed to see her in a summer garden, accented in the filtered light of a winery trellis.

Her smile was larger. Confidence squared her shoulders, and she held her head like a queen. *My queen.*

The gold of my ring on her finger glinted on her finger.

Yes, she should have more jewelry. But the solitary piece was a brand, a signal to the entire world that this woman was mine. Heir to a brutal legacy, and owner of my soul.

If I had one.

"We'll need travel clothes as well. Let her pick at least three outfits to tide us over until she can connect with her luggage."

My words made an eyebrow go up. I hadn't outright promised her she could talk to her sister, but I wouldn't rule it out. She wasn't my prisoner, but it was safer for everyone if she remained close. At least until I worked out an amicable solution with my hard-headed father.

Tonight's meal with him would not go well.

He had been the one to suggest my marriage to Dianora. An alliance between his banking and shipping interests and their multi-faceted empire would elevate him into legendary circles.

The world was not enough for some people.

At the time, I wasn't fighting the union, nor was I helping it along. I'd reached out to Dianora's brother mere days ago to suggest a solution that didn't result in marriage to his conniving sister.

And without any schemes on my part, I'd found one.

Of course, that didn't change the facts. Her brother, Adelmo, was dead. I was blamed for his demise, and to complicate things, my bride was *not* Dianora, but this golden siren with her forward, but humble, no-nonsense approach to life.

This respite came with strings. Ones my father was undoubtedly working on ways to manipulate.

Marrying Allie may have severed his current puppetry, but he was a master of diplomacy. A weapon so cruel and subtle, it was a challenge to outwit.

For that, I needed an ally. One who lived to keep my father under control. I left Allie to the whims of the stylist and reached out to the only other person who I trusted.

When he picked up the extension, I greeted him warmly. "Aiaiu." Grandfather. He was my mother's father. She had been his youngest and favorite child. And me? The spoiled son of a man who never answered for his transgressions.

"Mario. It has been too long since I've heard your voice."

"I'm sorry, Grandfather."

"You're never sorry. What ill wave washed you to your father's doorstep and not mine?"

Damn it. He *knew*. He was supposed to be retired and blissfully enjoying life outside of the family drama. "I married."

My grandfather made a harsh noise, one that told me he didn't like this change. I'd need to tread lightly.

"I would ask to introduce her to you."

His silence wasn't comforting. "The timing for your introduction is dire, I assume?"

It was. By now, the seasoned professionals in my circle would know I'd escaped the U.S. and landed here. And I was certain my father contacted Dianora's agents to press for another negotiation. Meanwhile, if Grandfather kept that close of an eye on the business, he'd *expect* me to come to him.

"Yes."

"I will leave today. Loppa will arrange a flight. It will spare you the stormy seas and winding roads. Both are filled with too many potholes and assassins." His tone was too abrupt to argue with.

"Be careful. They'll be watching the airports. The contract is twelve million as of last night. No one around me is safe."

He laughed. "My grandson, are you trying to compete with me? When I kidnapped your grandmother, the price was fourteen. And that was without inflation. Twelve. Ha!" With that, the line went dead.

I smiled at the memory of my grandmother. Both her and my mother were vibrant women, with a light inside that rarely dulled. Grandfather guarded them greedily and gave each a ring bearing his family crest. My grandmother was buried with hers.

The empty place on my pinky itched. I'd given my mother's ring to Allie. Right or wrong, I'd have to answer for that.

Firenze, Loppa's daytime replacement, knocked on the open door. "Your father wants to see you."

Of course he did. I joined him in his library. The small windows set deep in the wall barely revealed open sky. The meager light inside matched the overcast that had swept in overnight. I sat, not waiting for an invitation.

I shouldn't require one.

He steepled his fingers, assessing my weaknesses. "Where is your bride?"

"I left her with the fashion stylist."

Something calculating moved in the reflections in his eyes. "How much money are you planning to waste on that woman?"

"Not nearly as much as *your* choice would have cost me."

He frowned. "You found a peasant to replace the heir to one of the oldest families in Europe."

A soft tsk escaped my lips. I expected a dressing down, not direct insults. "Did you skip the background check on my wife?"

My father's face tightened. "Her ancestry doesn't change anything. American legacies are meaningless." His hand waved the thought away as if it were a pesky insect.

Careful, Father, your prejudice is showing. "And the old money in Europe is bound to too many headaches."

"Old money is *safe*. Non-volatile, and real." He pulled a page out of the stack of documents in front of him. "Four creditors, including your betrothed, have filed claims to your bride's wealth."

"Only four?" I would have thought the number higher.

"One is the U.S. Government. That should be enough to pauper her and her posterity for at least five generations."

This was about him, and *his* insecurities, not me or Allie. "How much do you owe Don Conti?"

My father stood up abruptly. "You do not talk to me like that!"

Right. God forbid anyone finds out a criminal family is

connected to the Minister of Trade. Would it be a surprise to anyone? He married my mother for those connections. He was attempting to marry me off for more connections.

"If you're so worried about money, you should have dug a little deeper into my *betrothed's* family." The Conti family was in debt. Urgent debt. And the loss of their heir apparent threatened to expose it.

I'd done *my* research. With my personal wealth and the family wealth, Dianora Conti could extinguish the rumors about her father's inconsistencies and her dead brother's ineptitudes.

In America, I'd offered to bail out Adelmo's debt in order to spare my family's fortune from Dianora's greedy clutches. But he was too timid to take my offer without talking to his father first.

And for that, everyone thought I'd taken his indecision as an insult. I hadn't. It was sheer chance he'd run that red light.

But whoever hit him didn't stick around. And that damned me.

My father paced. "Someone has to worry. I can't afford to simply *murder* anyone who irks me."

"Careful, Father. You might worry yourself into an early grave."

"I suppose you'd put me there?"

As tempting as the idea was, I would never do that. "That would be against the code." *Honor the family and your elders* were some of the first lessons.

His eyes narrowed. "Let me remind you that breaking a marriage contract goes against the code as well."

"I didn't offer a contract to the Contis, nor did I sign it." This was not my dishonor.

"You didn't have to," he reminded me. "All it took was my word."

"Yes, *yours*. Not mine." I leaned in to drive home a point that was sorely necessary. "My signature binds me to a different marriage contract. What a shame. You'll have to eat crow." I wasn't trying to be sarcastic, but my father's disrespect irritated me. He had only married into the family, therefore was not bound to the code.

My father had an answer at hand. He pulled a document from its binder. "The annulment agreement."

It dropped in front of me. I read the words and understood all too clearly the game afoot. I'd handed him the key myself. Father knew I wasn't in any shape to cement the union. He'd secured the doctor himself, not the family's more discreet physician.

Damn Ringo all to Hell. Without even wanting to, he'd delivered me to the noose. I needed to find him, convince him to lie about the timing of his attack. If it happened after the wedding, I could argue the marriage could not be annulled so easily. But what would that prove?

Nothing.

All my father needed to do was to hand Allie this piece of paper. The terms were clearly spelled out in both English and Italian. We hadn't consummated the marriage, and the annulment was as simple as signing on the dotted line.

My life, my fortune, and my fate was in the hands of a woman who barely knew me.

And with Allie's signature, she'd deliver me to someone

worse. My money was a side dish to Dianora's true intent. She adored power. Marrying me would consolidate her hold on the region.

And Dianora would demand heirs. Plural. At least two, in case one met an untimely demise like her brother had.

The thought of fucking that woman made me ill. Especially now that I'd tasted something sweet.

I placed both hands on his desk, being meticulous about their distance from the page staring at me. I stood up, using the leverage of leaning across the furniture to stare my father in the eye. "You're too late. I've slept with Allie."

The corner of his eye flinched. "Lie all you want. Until there's a grandchild, this marriage did not happen."

My fingers curled under, forming fists. "If there is a grandchild, you will never meet it." I didn't storm out. That would indicate I cared about him.

But I couldn't be in his presence any longer. I left him to his papers and diplomacy.

Loppa joined me on the terrace. He took point, scanning the surroundings for threats.

The rooftops of Milan spread out in a patchwork of old world and towering glass. The multiple spires of the Duomo poked upward with their marble saints stoically watching the city. The Maddonina glittered golden above them all. I stared at the shining symbol, wondering whether I'd always been my father's cat's-paw, or if this was some new torment I'd somehow earned through my lack of faith.

Loppa's low baritone broke into my musing. "It's cold up here."

I nodded, barely acknowledging his attempt to coax me

inside. I'd rested as much as I could, and was no longer burning up from the inside. Now, I prepared for a battle. My body might not yet be ready, but my mind was.

"Reach out to Ringo."

He stopped scanning the rooftops to scowl at me with confusion. "Why?"

"Because, if I know him well enough, he's probably secured my wife's sister and will be seeking a trade to draw me out. Set it up."

"Or, you could simply let your wife call her sister and find out if Ringo is with her. Then, cut his legs out from under him when you reunite them."

The prospect of hobbling Ringo brought joy to his face.

And I'll admit, the concept amused me, too. "I could."

"She'd appreciate it more than the clothing." He tipped his head at the penthouse.

His observation was astute.

"How much of the conversation with my father did you overhear?"

He grunted a short laugh and a quirked brow. "Enough."

I waited, because he had more to say.

"And if you're serious about your child never seeing that bastard, then you might want to *please* your wife. Otherwise…" He weighed one hand against the other and came up empty on both ends.

I shook my head and took a deep breath of the bracing air. My skin stung where Ringo cut me. A sign I shouldn't and couldn't be entertaining Loppa's fancy in the near future. But I was ready to leave this viper's den. "When is Don Manca due?"

He dipped his head. "After you stop making yourself sniper bait, I'll find out."

"While you're finding out, I'll be with my wife… *pleasing* her."

Loppa slapped me on the back, then led me by the neck into the penthouse. He'd done that to me when I was younger and he'd worked for my grandfather. Before he left, he slipped me Allie's phone. "This might help."

8

ALLIE

Dry cleaning and veterinary services were enemies. That's why I never abused my wallet on anything as exquisite as cashmere or silk. I stared at the rack of clothing and the detritus of my empty tote bag and fumed at the way everyone bulldozed over my wishes with calculated acquiescence.

My comfortable yoga pants were confiscated. The soft T-shirt I wore, gone. And like those things, my phone was no where to be found. I'd had it on the plane and put it in my bag. I surely had it last night. I fisted the charger in my hand and cursed my luck.

Mario entered. His face was paler, and his hair was windblown.

"Were you on the roof?" With a multi-million dollar bounty on his head. *Was he nuts?*

His head tipped as if to acknowledge my question. "The terrace."

He slowly curled into a soft chair. His body took time to settle, bracing against pain. I went to the pile on the bed and retrieved my bottle of acetaminophen. I spilled three tablets into my hand and passed them to him and then filled a glass with water.

He'd already popped the pills into his mouth and swallowed but accepted the water graciously. "Thank you."

"How bad is it?"

Mario shrugged. "I've had worse."

I hoped that was a lie but it sounded too much like the truth. Because his flippancy irritated me so, I mumbled sarcastically, "'Tis but a scratch."

His eyes darted to mine. A glint of amusement shown in them. Then it dimmed. "I have something of yours." He leaned so he wouldn't tweak his wound as he dug in his suit pocket. He handed my phone over without explanation.

I supposed criminals didn't feel the need to explain themselves.

Nor should I. I quickly dialed Ellie, mentally pulling up her itinerary. If all had gone well, she would have boarded the flight to Denver before noon. Passed through the final customs gate at three thirty, landed around seven this morning and checked into the first hotel in Venice. From there, I'd arranged for breakfast and a tour with a gondola ride later. But knowing my sister, she'd've gotten bored within a few minutes and diverted to the gondola first.

It rang four times. When she picked up, I could tell she was outside. "Did you make it to Venice?"

Instead of answering me, she asked, "Where are you? And where is my suitcase of underwear?"

Most of her risqué, brand-spanking-new underwear was still in its suitcase, conveniently still intact after the stylist's pillaging. The where question was a little trickier.

Should I tell her? I sent the question to Mario. He circled his hand, as if to say *go on* with it. "I'm in Milan."

"You couldn't get a flight to Venice? What the heck?"

"No, it was the only flight available at the time."

My sister brushed off the logistics easily. "Whatever. Just tell me what happened in as *few* words as possible."

A whole hell of a lot. "Where do you want me to start?" At saying "I do" or…?

"Did you get the refund from the wedding venue?"

"No. They didn't refund the money."

"I bet that dick Johnny is to blame for that, isn't he?"

"No."

"What do you mean, no?" Ellie shot back.

"It's complicated. Johnny hasn't bothered you, has he?" The last I'd seen of him, he was being hauled off to the emergency room thanks to Mario. That should have been a red flag, but I'd conveniently ignored it.

Mario raised an eyebrow as if it would help him listen in on my call easier.

"I haven't seen him. Thank God for small favors."

"Good." That was one less problem to deal with.

"Listen, I know you had to deal with my mess. I didn't even realize how bad it was until I got to the airport and tried to cash in the ticket. And, you got so delayed because of it, you didn't come back to the hotel. I'm *so* sorry."

"It's okay, El. I'm good."

"Really? I have *your* suitcases. Your itineraries and reservations…" My twin didn't sound convinced.

"I obtained clothes." And as far as itineraries went, those took second place to a hitman's bounty on my…*husband's* head. Even thinking about it that way made me embarrassed.

There was a beat of silence on the other end. "You… Miss 'I wear shit-covered boots' as a fashion statement. You've squirreled away every penny of Grandpa Pulaski's money, but bought clothes? In Milan?" The latter portion of that sounded just as incredulous as it possibly could.

But technically, I didn't buy the clothes. And Ellie would never let me hear the end of it if I told her I'd gotten married to a gangster who whisked me away in a private jet and bought me a wardrobe that outshone all my prior clothing purchases ten-fold. "Well, it was either that or freeze. It is February."

"Yeah, I thought it would be warmer for some reason. I should have stayed in Vegas. I'm shivering my lady nuts off here."

A masculine snort sounded from her end of the call.

"Are you with someone?"

Ellie never could lie to me well, so I heard the pitch change and the slight hesitation as she made up a lie. "Oh, that's just my interpreter. Don't mind him."

"You hired an interpreter?" I knew damn well she wouldn't know where to begin to do that. Ten bucks she met someone at a hotel bar and dragged him around Italy with her.

Mario leaned forward to eavesdrop better.

And reminded me I shouldn't be judgmental. Like, at all. I quickly switched the subject. "Have you talked to Mom?"

"No. It's crazy how she isn't blowing up my phone over the whole wedding being called off. You're a miracle worker."

Ah shit. I was walking the tightrope between busted and guilty. Fall on one side and never be trusted again. Fall on the other, and I'd never be believed again. Which was worse? I opted for the truth. Ellie wouldn't believe it anyway.

"So… about the wedding."

"Thank you for running interference with Mom. I bet she made you live stream the opera singer anyway, right?"

Yeah, that happened. "I met someone."

Dead, fucking silence. Finally, my sister squeaked out, "I'm sorry, *what?*"

"On the way to the chapel, I met someone." The words didn't want to come out right.

An ugly sound farted out of my sister's mouth. "You?" The laugh started as she spoke and didn't end.

"Yes. Me." *Damn her.*

"Woooo… I mean… who?" She gasped. "Wait, don't tell me, you ended up canceling the ride share, took the monorail, and he's one of the lion tamers at MGM."

"No." What kind of person did she think I was?

"Okay, a… banker?"

"No, but his dad is." *Supposedly.* I mouthed, "a banker" to Mario who had squinted at my side of the conversation when I mentioned *Il Bastardo.*

"Come on, *really*, Allie, you can't tease me like this. What does this mystery man do? Does he even exist? Is he a homeless guy who was hurt or something? Maybe he had a little dog you couldn't say no to?"

Her mockery was digging too deeply to ignore. All my life she'd made fun of my kindness toward anything in pain.

I chanced a glance at Mario, who was perched atop the chair like a throne, but favoring his wound. And the fact that she was hitting so close to the truth, except maybe for the whole dog part, pissed me off. So, I decided to lay some unvarnished truth bombs right at her feet. "He's in international business. You know, the *Family* kind. And might even be a—"

Mario leaned forward abruptly and lifted a finger in the air as if I had one chance not to screw this up. I felt his warning almost as clearly as if he'd touched my lips with that finger. Because of that and because Ellie would notice my pause too soon, I finished with, "—a great kisser… if he wasn't such a stick in the mud."

"Oh, now that sounds like something you'd do."

My sister was a dead woman. "What do you mean by that?"

"Nothing. I mean… well, there was that *doctor*."

I frowned. She would have to bring him up. I had no defense readied.

"Or, the insurance adjuster."

"No. He doesn't count. In my defense, I broke that off almost as soon as he detailed his lettuce allergy… and his peanut allergy…"

"Don't forget the big one, allergic to…*animals*."

"I shouldn't have worn my work coat to the date."

"I wish I could have been a fly on that restaurant wall."

"Good thing he carried his epi-pen," I mused.

"So, does Mr. *International Business* like animals?"

I glanced at Mario who'd amused himself by pretending he wasn't listening in anymore. "I don't know."

"What do you mean you don't know? Ask. Duh."

I covered the little hole at the end of the phone and did just that. "Do you like animals?"

Mario looked at me curiously. "Better than most people."

Good enough. I relayed the statement to Ellie.

"What's his name, how tall is he, and does he have any children? Oh, wait, forget I asked that. You'd be too busy taking care of them to call me."

While I gnawed on the worry bone of whether he had children or a prior relationship looming in the not-so-distant past, I answered what I could. "His name is Mario, and he's kind of tall." And dark, and handsome…with pouty lips and a knowingly sharp gaze that didn't miss a thing. His cheek dimpled slightly.

Ellie broke the spell that little divot was casting over me. "Mario. Like the video game? It-za *me*, Mario!"

I'd lay odds her voice echoed around the canals. "I'm hanging up."

"No, don't. I'm sorry." A giggle leaked out which ruined the apology. I knew her well enough she wanted to say it again just to get it out of her system.

"You wouldn't say it that way to his face. Trust me."

"What? Like he's *dangerous*? I'm sorry, but there's no way

my sister hooked up with someone dangerous. No freaking way."

Not only hooked up with, married. "Here's the short version. Mom loved the wedding. Aunt Susan cried. And I'll lay odds that Dad is going to have to listen to opera for a whole month. You did good by picking that theme."

"Wait. You…"

"Got married. Yes."

A loud noise made me pull the phone away from my ear. If I didn't know better, I'd guess it was the sound of plastic and glass hitting something hard. But I couldn't ask because the call went dead.

I stared at the screen for a long moment.

"She's with someone?"

Mario's question shouldn't have bothered me, but it did. "Listen, it's not as bad as it sounds. I know my sister. She's not flighty and…" Who was I kidding? She was going to marry a wanna-be gangster up until she saw the dirt on him our family lawyer sent. And right after finding out, stormed out of the room in the middle of the afternoon to get shit-faced drunk… in her wedding dress, not caring what kind of scene she made. That wasn't flighty, that was… jilted.

Mario caught on to my thoughts quickly and sent me a commiserative question in his expression. But I had more than enough doubts of my own.

"Do you think I should I be worried?"

Very carefully, he moved closer and knelt so he could rest a hand on my knee. "Do you want me to put someone on her? For protection, I mean?"

"You can do that?"

He nodded gently.

The debate in my head went like this. *Yes, oh my God, please?* And, *I shouldn't bother because Ellie survived this far without help. Not only that, but she was stubborn if she was being forced to do something.* And finally, the rampant thoughts coalesced into a singular question. *What kind of man had I married?*

He was connected enough to have a private plane whisk us away to Italy. He was related to a top member of the Italian government. Well-off enough to afford not only expensive fashion, but royalty-worthy fashion.

And, he was good-looking, considerate, and most of all, brutally dangerous. The type of man who could choose anyone in the world. And he was kneeling at my feet.

"Why did you marry me?" I was nothing but an unemployed veterinarian with a zany twin. I wasn't a supermodel, or a talented actress, or anything that a man like him would want. I was…punctual…utilitarian. What an endorsement. *Not.*

His face softened. Maybe it started at the eyes, or in the little twitch of relaxation by his mouth. Or in the round pads of his lips. But it was there, kindness, then humor that crinkled the skin next to his eyes. "I married you for a limo ride." He blushed and let the moment slip into uncomfortable silence. Too soon, the smile on his face dropped, and he placed his hand on his wound, holding the pain in.

Maybe even the action was to hold his thoughts in. Lie through omission or hide behind humor. Ellie did that, too. Had she learned that from me?

I decided it was better we not fool ourselves. "I married

you because my parents wanted to see a wedding and I really didn't want to create a scene."

He closed his eyes as if the confession hurt.

"But…I kind of want to stay married to see if we…"

His eyes snapped open, sharp and intense. He waited for me to continue.

It was hard to admit, but I liked him. Not just because he was wounded, or because he tried to hide the vulnerability, like all creatures with fears do, but because I sensed underneath all the glitz and the trappings of his world, and despite the oddity of our circumstances, that he was a careful man. Solid. The kind who valued loyalty and didn't trust lip service, but instead, looked for the actions behind any worthless words by judging the deeds a person does.

Mario was the kind of person who didn't suffer cowards or fools, or depended on anyone who couldn't prove their worth. And somehow, I *should* be worthy because he'd deemed it so.

In spite of my doubts, I continued. "I think we might fit. Maybe I'm wrong. But I believe we should find out."

The smile on his face started with a hesitant flicker. Then his lips thinned slightly. But they softened, and the smile grew. The dimples on his face dug deep and remained in place while he silently accepted my answer.

"I'd be honored to have that opportunity."

Why was my heart beating so fast? He hadn't said anything earth-shattering or romantic.

But it felt momentous.

9

MARIO

Seduction is a delicate art form. One I never paid much attention to. It wasn't logical. Nor was it an exact science. What worked in one instance may fail in another. That alone should have been enough to entice me to test methodologies and refine my approach.

Yet, I was at a loss. Allie, as pragmatic as she was, held herself open to knowing me.

That frightened me.

Not because I feared her. I was afraid of myself. At least of what she would find as she uncovered who I was underneath the armor I presented the world. Perhaps the true terror would be uncovering that I was truly heartless. I'd worked so hard to prove my worth to the family, to my father, to the people who depended on my expertise, that I'd destroyed my ability to love.

Underneath all of that echoed the words I spit at my father. I regretted them, and they hung on my mind like weights. Or like a sword ready to slice through the fragile offer of hope I might be able to out maneuver my father. I'd be a fool not to grasp this opportunity.

If I were physically able to, that is.

Hiding my disability drained me. Yet pretending my wound didn't hurt didn't work on my new wife. She was too trained in physiology to ignore the silent ways I broadcast my pain.

"You need to rest," she observed.

I studied her. "I need to know more about your sister, her itinerary, and her habits. It will help Loppa find her faster."

"Only if you lie down. I will not have you straining yourself. Come on." She held out a hand.

Such fine fingers. I marveled at their beauty, and strength. My wife was a delicate woman, yet not fragile. And, she was a stubborn soul. I let her pull me off my knees. She was gentle with me. Not doing much more than a tug, but offering a bent arm to lean on as we climbed the grand staircase in my father's home. Loppa trailed behind in the shadows, aware of our location, but providing an illusion of privacy.

One Allie saw through. She addressed him. "Come on, I'm not repeating myself, nor letting him out of my sight."

Loppa grinned and took a chair by the door as Allie laid out the plans she'd set for her sister's honeymoon.

They were impressive. She'd accommodated for nearly everything and created contingencies to meet her sister's tastes and mercurial moods. I could use someone like her on logistics.

What was I thinking?

Surely, she'd run to the hills, or the authorities if she knew my real profession. It was one thing to be part of a global operation, but fully another to be their sinister weapon when traditional methods failed.

I counted the carved squares in the ceiling as she spelled out everything Loppa needed to know about the sudden plan changes her sister might make. Once she finished, I reminded him of what was at stake.

"This man she's with must not harm her. Understood?"

Loppa grinned. "I'll take him out if I have to."

Allie's mouth opened. "That's a little—"

"Necessary. I'm certain Loppa understands what she means to you, and how far he can carry his actions."

"All I really need to know is that she's safe, has everything she needs, and is enjoying herself. And, maybe join her."

There was a note of longing in her voice.

"You've never been to Italy before, have you?" I asked.

"No."

"You planned on being here with her?"

"No, I didn't. But when she canceled the wedding, I… well, it isn't every day you get to go to somewhere like this. Right?"

I sat up, prepared to adjust my plans. But Allie rushed to the bed and coaxed me to rest.

That was something I would not do. I held her hand and told Loppa to take care of locating her sister, and to plan an exodus from my father's cage. Too soon, my father would figure out a way to trap me in his webs. And when that happened, I needed to be somewhere else.

When he exited, I confessed, "I can't sleep."

Allie put a hand on my chest. "You don't have to sleep, just rest. Got it?"

There was one way I could do that. If she stayed with me. I covered her hand with my own. "Keep that there. But tell me, if you had to design a trip for yourself, what would it entail?"

She thought for a long time. The silence was soothing. But there was a pucker between her brows I didn't like. So, I reminded her, "Remember, this would be *only* for you."

Allie nodded, firming up the plans in her mind. "I'd want to visit places that aren't over-hyped. Art and architecture are great, but I want to get to know the people. How they live, how their ancestors lived. See things that aren't in the guide book. Eat the real food, not the touristy stuff. I'm not interested in the parties and costumes, and that sort of thing."

"I'm not either."

She tipped her head to inspect my face. "That's hard to believe. You seem so..."

Instead of voicing her true thoughts, she kept them inside. I didn't want that.

"Insult me."

"No."

I smiled. "You want to."

"No, I don't. Although, I believe you may take offense."

"Offend me then."

She quirked up a brow, as if testing my resolve. But I wanted the truth.

"Please. I give you permission."

"See? There it is. You're… you've got an aristocratic air. It's not nearly as pronounced as your father's, but it's there. You're urbane. I'm… not."

"I'm only that way when I have to be. This place brings it out whether I want it or not."

Her smile was tight. "I think you were trained to be that way, and can't help it."

There was truth in that. "You haven't seen my—"

What was I doing? Confessing that I had a brutal nature?

"Your what?"

"My rural side." And if she stayed with me, she would see it all. Then I'd have to—

Her smile got wider. "You don't have a rural side."

On the contrary, I preferred the quiet life of the farmland over the city. "Let's test that, shall we? Have you ever milked a goat?"

"Yes. Have you ever delivered lambs in the spring?"

"At least once."

"Really? Where?"

That triggered a fond memory. "On Grandfather's farm. The family has a villa in the mountains of Sardinia. His sons, his nephews, the grandchildren including me, all learned how to move the flock from the summer pastures to the homestead and back. It was a rite of passage—a good one."

"You were a shepherd?"

"Amongst other things. "Is that hard to believe?"

She traced my brow with her fingertips. "Did you have any pets there?"

"A few. Mostly working dogs, but there are barn cats. Although, they are *not* pets. I believe they think they own the farm and we were merely their minions."

Allie laughed. "I've known a few like that."

Ah yes, her profession. "Tell me about your job."

Her face froze.

Now who was hiding secrets?

"What part of being a vet do you like?"

"When the animals get better."

As opposed to the times they obviously did not stay that way. I brushed one of the locks of hair that had fallen into her face aside. "What part don't you like?"

Her face tightened. "Not being good enough to fix everything."

I brought her fingers to my lips and kissed the tips. We were alike in certain ways. The reason Ringo was as good of an assassin as he was could be attributed to planning and preparation. Which was my strongest contribution to our system. His betrayal hurt. Worse? I wondered if he resented me. I'd done my best to make him the most feared and ruthless killer he could be.

But in doing so, had I created a monster capable of hating me?

"Allie?" I wanted to kiss her.

"I was fired."

What? "From your job?"

She nodded slowly. "It wasn't because anything I did. It

was my grandfather. His money…the clients." Her mouth turned down. "The firm couldn't have a mobster's granddaughter tending to the children's puppies, right?"

"*They were idiots.*"

"I think I understand what you just said."

I grinned. "It wouldn't take much to figure out." I broke down the words for her.

She repeated them back to me.

They were. "*Kiss me.*"

"I don't know that one."

"Yes, you do." Instead of translating, I slipped my hand around the tender curve of her neck and tugged her close.

"*Kiss me,*" I whispered.

Our lips met, the touch so soft I thought I imagined it. But Allie groaned and the vibration shot from my lips to my groin.

Screw caution and tenderness and all that foolishness. I needed this woman. My grip clenched in her hair and I strained upward to deepen the kiss.

And regretted it instantly.

She broke the kiss. "You're not resting."

"*And you are making me work too damn hard for a simple kiss.*"

"What was that about a kiss?"

Her Italian was improving. "Lie next to me." I shifted to give her room.

"No…that's dangerous."

I laughed. "Truly, it is not."

"What about your code?"

I paused. The temptation to say, "screw the code," was forefront. But she reminded me that I'd promised not to pressure her. Yet there was a loophole. "We are married. It is…acceptable. Should you *want* to rest with me. Do you?"

Her smile was cagey. "I think you're trying to trick me."

"Me? Never." I was such a terrible liar.

Without breaking eye contact, Allie placed one knee on the bed, then the other. Gracefully, she slipped into the space next to me. "You will not strain yourself, agreed?"

"*There is no such thing as strain when you make love.*"

Her eyebrow went up. "I think I know what that meant. In English, you…naughty man."

"I will not strain myself."

"You're such a liar."

It was good we were on the same page. Slowly, I turned to be face to face with her. She'd tucked her hands in front of her, like a prayer. I pulled the top one away and laid it against my heart. "Listen with your fingertips."

This close, her perfume was a secondary note to the sensuous warmth of her body. In that heat was the essence of her, my queen, my life, my…

I had a wife.

And she was beautiful. All I had to do was touch her, please her…woo her. My heart beat faster.

I traced her eyebrow first, starting slowly, then trailing my fingers along her tender cheekbones and along the fine hairs curling by her ear. I traced that shell, finding out she was ticklish. The arch that formed the top curve was the most sensitive. It caused her to curl protectively with one shoulder closer. But along the bottom, she relaxed and let me explore.

In retaliation, she traced my face, starting with my lips.

The sensation shot to my gut and despite the tensing of my muscles, it was magical. Yet, I couldn't stand the torture long. I nipped at the pad of her finger to warn her away.

"He bites."

"Are you surprised?"

She caught the soft curve of her lower lip between her teeth momentarily. I kissed the pinched flesh.

"You are an exceptional kisser." Her breathy voice was music to my ears.

"I must have removed that stick up my ass."

She reared back. "Oh. I'm sorry I said that."

"Forgiven. Come back. I want to kiss you again."

"You do?" That curious spot between her brows tightened.

"Very much."

The hesitation and the movement as she swallowed warned me she didn't trust me enough.

"*I won't bite.*"

"Now I know you're lying."

"I thought you didn't understand."

Her expression turned mischievous. "Cats bite. Dogs bite. A lot of animals bite. And when I learned Latin I learned that word. Unless it means something else?"

I smiled, trying to keep my secrets from her. "Do you understand this?" I kissed her deeply.

She gasped, and I pulled her close. In the breaths between kisses, I traced her skin, then her body. The soft fabric of her clothing didn't hide the lovely curves and shape of my bride.

In turn, she unbuttoned my shirt, revealing my skin and

giving her access to scrape her fingers across my chest. The light scratch of her nails urged me to tear her clothing off and make love to her with a fury that boiled in my soul.

Yet, I kept to my promise not to strain myself. Slowly, I unbuttoned her shirt until she matched me, save for the exquisite lingerie she wore underneath. I traced the embroidery on the fabric that cupped her breasts. "My compliments to the stylist."

Allie's skin flushed pink. "This isn't… I mean, my sister packed these. I don't normally wear anything this fancy."

Fancy or not, I should remove it. Perhaps toss it somewhere it would get "lost." Then I would be forced to spoil her rotten and buy my wife custom lingerie. I slipped my hand under her open shirt to find the closure.

A knock on the door interrupted us. Loppa peeked in. His face was a ruddy color as he tried not to look at Allie scrambling to right her clothes.

"Forgive me, Don Valentini, Signora Valentini." Loppa's head dipped. "Don Manca has arrived."

10

ALLIE

Matrimonio all'improvviso, o inferno o paradiso. —
A sudden marriage [is] either heaven or hell.

At first glance, Mario's grandfather appeared harmless enough. Of course, my own grandfather was the same way. Slightly stooped, deep wrinkles around the corners of his eyes and fainter worry lines grooving his forehead. Don Manca's face spoke of a long life. Although, his was much more weathered and less urbane than Mario's father's.

This was the man who'd taught Mario about his rural life, and I wanted to sit under a shaded tree with him and talk of nothing but bread and lambs for days.

But I didn't miss the way he froze when Mario and I emerged downstairs. His sharp gaze took in our closeness, the subtle way I curved my arm under his to provide support, and the silence where there were loud voices only moments before.

Don Valentini was less guarded about his open disgust. Of course, it was tinted with a bit of… smugness? He reveled in the awkwardness.

"Nipotino." The warmth in Don Manca's address was evident. I glanced at Mario to see his reaction. A genuine smile spread across his face and he shook off my arm to hug his grandfather.

"Buonasera, Nonno. Che piacere vederti!"

"È passato troppo tempo! Questa signora non è la tua fidanzata. Sei pazzo?"

I looked to Mario for a translation.

Instead, he introduced me. "Don Manca, grandfather, this is my wife, Allie Jacobs now Valentini."

His father winced.

"Matrimonio all'improvviso, o inferno o paradiso," Don Manca muttered. Marriage, improvised… something…heaven or hell. Damn. He didn't like me one bit.

Mario ignored his outburst and continued, "Allie, this is my grandfather, Don Manca."

"A pleasure to meet you. Mario speaks fondly of you," I said.

One eyebrow went up. "He speaks secrets?"

"Only about sheep." I tried to smile, but the unwavering scrutiny was almost worse than his father's deliberate cold shoulder.

"Do you like sheep?"

"When they aren't trying to knock me over, yes."

He laughed. "They all *try*. The trick is to never turn your back on them."

"I'll remember that."

"Allie is a veterinary surgeon," Mario confided.

An out of work one, but I wasn't going to mention that.

"Say it is a lie. This beautiful woman?"

"Sì, Aiaiu."

Don Manca glanced at Mario's left side. Apparently, he knew about the injury. I shot a glance to the corner where Loppa lurked. He quickly looked away. *Guilty.*

There were low words I couldn't decipher. Mario's father turned his head sharply and cocked it as if trying to figure out what was spoken. Apparently, it wasn't Italian, or a dialect so strong he couldn't make it out.

One Mario had no difficulty with. "Sì, Aiaiu. She knows."

All humor fled from Don Manca's face. His silence stretched for too long. Eventually, Mario dipped his head, as if caught doing something wrong.

I straightened my shoulders. I would not apologize for helping Mario, nor would I attempt to hide the truth. I slipped my arm back under Mario's, lending him strength.

As I did, the scrutiny refocused on me.

Don Manca scanned me from head to toe. His eyes caught on the ring on my finger. The tension in his jaw made the wrinkles deepen. More low words to Mario, mostly unkind if his tone was any indication.

Mario shook his head. "I made my choice."

Don Manca squinted at me then. "Your grandfather, Albert, do you remember him?"

"Yes, I was ten when he moved to Nevada. We visited when he came to town. He liked walnuts, and played a mean game of Euchre. That's a card game which is popular where I grew up."

"He played a mean game of Scopa, too."

He knew my grandfather. I froze. Suddenly the danger Mario was in became a little *too* real.

Don Manca ignored my panic and carried on. "Albert was the best with numbers. Yours, his, it didn't matter. Give him odds or transfers, and that man was a magician."

Don Valentini cleared his throat.

"Someone's jealous." Mario's grandfather laughed at his jibe. He shot a quick, "Don't worry, the man is dead," to Don Valentini. Then his attention refocused on Mario, and then me. "You two will make magnificent children. I should hope to live to see a hundred and twenty, just to witness them come of age." He leaned a little to confide in me. "I turned ninety-seven this year." His eyes wrinkled at the corners, but the distance in his eyes was palpable. "There are eight centenarians in our village. Three years I'll be lucky number nine." He wagged his fingers in the air as if to say, "Watch me. I'll beat all of them."

"Don Manca, if you are done, we need to talk." Don Valentini's interruption was not subtle. His nod included Mario, but not me.

"I've said what I needed to say about the matter. My *wife* and I will retire until dinner." Mario turned to lead me away, but his father had other plans.

"This cannot wait."

Even Don Manca took offense. "It absolutely *can* wait. My grandson is newly married. Business will wait."

"This business cannot."

Despite being shorter than Don Valentini, Don Manca squared off in front of him. Loppa took three steps out of the corner and watched for any threats.

Don Manca shook a finger in front of his son-in-law's face. "When you married my daughter I did not ask for your loyalty, but you agreed to allow her and any of her children to remain loyal to me, *only* me. Did you forget?"

"I did not."

"Then *your* business waits."

Don Valentini hesitated, but then dipped his head. "Of course." He took two steps back before turning to leave the room.

However, the tension didn't dissipate. The anger in Don Manca's eyes fixed on the doorway his son in law departed from. He mused aloud in English so I'd overhear. "Mario is my youngest daughter's child. Her mother was my third wife. I'd divorced one, and buried another before I married his grandmother. And she was the one great love of my life." He turned to face me. "*Remember* this when you prop him up to play his father's show pony. He is *all* I have left of her."

He motioned for my hand, the one with the ring on it. Age or emotion made his hands shake as he lifted the emblem closer to get better light on it. "This was one of two rings ever made with this seal. One is buried with my wife." His sharp eyes met mine. "My grandson is not a foolish man. But I fear Death has tapped his shoulder and muddled his mind. Do not be his downfall. I will not forgive that."

"Don Manca," Mario tried to reason with him.

"No. Do not cajole me. This is not a game." He gripped my hand hard. "You made this woman your *wife*. And with this ring, you swore there would be no other while you both live."

That declaration was awful, scary, and tragic. What if I was just a fevered bad decision? What if—

"There is no other for me."

Oh, Mario. I wanted to plead with him to walk that back for his sake. I also wanted terribly for his words to be true, forever. I *wanted* to be his one great love. But we weren't even close to making that choice yet.

Don Manca dropped my hand. "I hope you are not lying to me." With that, he motioned for Loppa to follow him.

"Was that a shit show, or was it just my imagination?"

Mario's exhale was heavy. "It went about as well as I expected."

Great. At least one of us planned for this. "More rest. Real rest this time."

Mario's lips curved upward.

"I mean it."

He shot me a sly look and held out his hand. "Death has tapped me on the shoulder."

In response, the sound I made wasn't pleasant. It revealed all my frustration and perhaps a small amount of the terror coursing through me. "That's enough of that talk. You are *not* dying today."

"You've never attended one of Father's formal dinners then."

Was that a joke?

God, I hoped it was.

THE VALENTINI FAMILY'S PENTHOUSE WAS LIKE THOSE LITTLE nested Russian dolls. Every layer of it was luxurious, but more of the same pristine, exquisite sterility with a touch of color or splash of ostentatiousness that screamed money.

This layer, a grand dining room with attending kitchens and gathering salons, was a study in cream and gold with large windows showcasing the city's majestic northern half. The view was dominated by skyscrapers framed by the faint peaks of the Alps in the distance. And like the layers above, there was a splash of color. This time the color was a deep royal blue in the velvet cushions of the ivory seating.

Mario's father must like blue. I logged that for later reference and searched for any familiar face in the crush. There were over two dozen in attendance because the long table had place settings for thirty guests with its gold trimmed fine china, gilt-toned dinnerware, gold chargers, and fresh camellia centerpieces staggered every four feet down its impressive length.

Mario slipped his arm under mine. I almost switched the position back, but he captured my hand with his and leaned in. "This way I don't telegraph weakness, and you are guarding my side."

That made tactical sense. Although with my hand trapped so well, I couldn't do more than nod and smile while he made introductions. Luckily, most of the guests noted his possessiveness with a nervous smile and perhaps a knowing wink or two.

"Who's the show pony now?"

Mario smiled, and a small laugh leaked out. "You look beautiful tonight. It's difficult to resist parading you in front of Father's guests."

The muted sage gown was one of the more elegant pieces chosen for me. But I regretted that I hadn't gone with something more flashy. I was outclassed by the embossed damask wallpaper.

Or that necklace…I'd never seen diamonds that big in real life. The woman wearing it was practically a secondary attraction in her deep amethyst velvet gown and supermodel sleek looks.

A flash of red snagged my attention. It attracted Mario's as well. A striking woman in crimson satin strode toward us as if there were no one else in the room. Her eyes were fixed on me. In them, I could almost see the ways she wanted to dismember me.

His grip on my hand got a little tighter. "Stay at my side."

In spite of his hissed warning, he plastered a smile on his face. "Dianora, it's a rare exception to see you at my father's home." His words didn't match the guarded tone.

My heart rate picked up, likely triggered by the predatory way she scanned me from head to toe. Without more than that introduction, she hated me. *Why?*

"Hardly rare. Your father welcomes me and my family at his soirees. It is *you* who eludes capture religiously. I'm certain that's a skill which has kept you alive lately." Her smile flashed wickedly before she continued. "And this particular event is rife with rumors about your latest indiscretions. I can't wait to see what kind of… entertainment… there is in store for us tonight." Her lips puckered into a little moue, telegraphing disappointment more than excitement.

She is a liar, my intuition whispered.

And worse? There was a history between Mario and Dianora. One I couldn't begin to prepare for because the "entertainment" had already begun. I could practically hear the out of tune strains of a macabre circus playing in my head.

Would it be awful to flash the ring? Yes, it totally would.

But that didn't stop me from placing my left hand over Mario's too-tight grip on my right hand. It made a cozy sandwich with my only piece of jewelry as armor to guard him from her evil clutches.

Her eyes dipped and noted the emblem in the flat oval of gold. Instantly, the skin around her eyes tightened and her eyes narrowed. One eyebrow went up as she met my eyes. "You work fast."

Mario moved between us. "When Death smiles in your face, you learn how to move quickly."

Almost willfully, she relaxed and smiled. "That is nothing new. You make dancing with death a habit, dear Mario. That's not a wise choice." Her outstretched hand brushed his arm as she pretended to offer him a different path.

Her words were uttered with an air of superiority and familiarity I couldn't hope to match. Ever.

"Allie, my bride, this is Dianora Conti, heir to her family's fortune after the untimely demise of her brother, Adelmo. An unfortunate event barely even a week past. Yet she wears red tonight."

That told me a hell of a lot in very few words.

"And Dianora, this is my wife, Allie, formerly Jacobs, of Chicago. She's one of Albert Pulaski's grandchildren. Did your father once work with him? I seem to recall he may have held some capital in an overseas conglomerate. I personally know Adelmo had dealings with that company since. Perhaps you two have common business interests?"

Dianora's eyelids lowered, shielding her thoughts. But that didn't matter. The way her chin went up at the mention of her brother, again, didn't speak of grief, unless she was in the anger phase.

Considering the carefully bitten words being shot back and forth between Mario and her, that could be true.

Her white teeth caught the overhead light as she forced a smile. "You shield yourself admirably, Mario. But all the riches in the world won't stop my father's vengeance. He'll want to see his son's killer dead. No foreign relationships or family heirlooms can protect you from what is coming. And now that I have heard from your own lips that my dear brother discussed business with you before he was murdered, well… Father will need to know that information, won't he?" Her smile grew more poisonous. "What is the price on your head at now, I wonder? Was it, fifteen million? Or perhaps twenty?"

Mario hadn't taken his eyes off her. I didn't dare move because this was a battle of two apex predators. I was simply the human gazelle caught unawares between them as they squared off. It had been foolish to flash the ring. In that silly act of jealousy, I hadn't staked my claim, I'd stepped into the line of fire.

11

MARIO

The table sat thirty. A dozen chairs each squeezed together on the long sides while three odd chairs graced each end. My father, in typical fashion, set himself in the king's chair nearest the center of the dozen facing the best view. Opposite him was one of his blander political allies, but the far ends were reserved for his primary foes or bitterest allies. Quadrants were drawn. My father clustered useful allies or assets nearest to him, staggered between guests of varying power or beauty.

His counterpart across the table was sandwiched between their rival's wife, a formidable force in her own right, and the wife of a wealthy businessman. The rival on his far right held court with a race car driver and a leading fashion house maven. Flanking them were two men of high status. That would be a boring conversation, but endlessly fruitful for them, no doubt.

On the opposite end, were men of infinitely more

power. Don Manca leading the charge with a wealthy Greek financier at his side. With a deft move, I captured the card at Don Manca's right hand, and placed my card next to Allie's place on the corner. The poor soul who'd lost his card was stuck next to Dianora.

Between the antipasto and primo, I collected Allie's hand and pulled it to my lips. The ring on her finger was warm as my kiss brushed it. I lingered there, savoring her skin and the beauty that was my bride. As I did, I played with her fingers, positioning them so the table would glimpse the gold adornment on her left hand.

"You're being obvious," Allie noted.

"I am?"

She nodded, a smile playing on her lips. "I'm beginning to think you plan farther ahead than I do."

If she only knew. "It's called plotting against enemies. And I'm *very* good at it."

The words carried across the table, and Dianora's eyes narrowed.

"What he isn't good at is honoring contracts."

Her words carried, creating little ripples of reaction in their wake. She pointedly toyed with a large diamond ring on her finger I hadn't noticed before.

Allie leaned to me and quietly asked, "What did she say?"

"Does your lady friend not understand Italian? How… rustic." Dianora smiled and switched to Greek to address the financier. *"To think, Americans go their entire lives learning only one language. It puts them at a disadvantage, don't you agree?"*

Once she convinced the man to be her accomplice, she

shot a barb in Allie's direction, switching between languages with ease. *"Do you know any German? French? Russian perhaps? Or even the lovely Greek language this esteemed friend of our families speaks?"*

The man smiled at her compliment.

"She's mocking me, isn't she?" Allie's whispered question didn't beg for an answer.

Dianora laughed and whispered to her friend.

He piped up, "Charles the Fifth was once rumored to say, 'If I had to speak with God, I would do so in Spanish, because the language of the Spaniards radiates seriousness and majesty; if I speak with friends, it is in Italian, because the language of the Italians is intimate; if I need to flatter someone, in French, because there is nothing more flattering than their language.' But it was Marcus Aurelius who said, 'If the Gods speak, they will surely use the language of the Greeks.'"

Dianora beamed. "Such brilliant phrases. I only know a quaint one my father spoke often. *'Wife and oxen from your own country.'* All else brings trouble."

Don Manca cleared his throat and spoke in his heavily accented Gallurian dialect. *"Mario, tell that Tuscan bitch to shut up and pass the bread."* Then he switched to English. "Speaking of oxen, my grandson's *wife* is an animal doctor."

Nervously, Allie confirmed to the curious guests that yes, she was a licensed veterinarian and fielded a follow-up question with ease.

"Was that how you met? Tending to a *beast's* injuries?" Dianora skewered me with her glare.

Allie paled and shot a panicked glance at me, giving our secrets away.

"We met when I stole her cab."

Her eyes dropped to her plate, but she smiled. "It was a ride share. And I don't know how you ended up at the same destination."

"He wouldn't take me where I wanted to go. Claimed he couldn't reset the route."

"Really?"

"It's true."

Her little huh of surprise was cute. "Someone stood up to you?"

"No, he was too panicked to think of anything else. I'm lucky he was so flustered."

"I stole your grandmother's best milk cow and five goats. I ransomed them back to her father to buy her hand in marriage."

Allie laughed and smiled at Don Manca. "That's so… roguish. And, sweet. I see where he gets his behavior from." Her eyes drifted to me, and I was caught in their colors.

Mostly, they picked up the pale, earthy green of her dress. My heart drowned out the conversation around us. My senses were tuned solely to her.

The service setting down the tiny servings of cheese and fruit startled me.

"That's all it took? A stolen car?" The Greek asked.

"No, we… later we attended an opera performance." Allie's amusement almost gave her lie away.

"And a masquerade," I added.

"That mask was so sexy." Allie traced my face where the half-mask had ended. Her finger drifted down to my lips. "And we kissed."

"Yes." The memory of her lips trembling against mine transfixed me, bewitched me. It entangled me in spells I had no defenses for. "That is when I decided to make you my queen."

"Lovely, but a bit sudden, no? I mean last week your father was in talks with my father to finalize our engagement contract."

Dianora's words and the way she rolled her left hand in the air to show off the diamond on her finger silenced one half of the table. They'd traveled far enough that my father cut off his conversation mid-sentence and glared down the expanse. But it didn't land on her. It landed on Allie and me.

Whispers started up in the background. Little titters built into the glamour of wicked birds who valued gossip over substance.

Allie's eyes went wide and moisture flooded the edges.

I needed to halt the damage before she bolted. She had that look—one of utter devastation, and terror. I stood up, holding my hand out for hers to hold. Once I was sure of my grip, I spoke loud enough for the entire room could hear my words clearly as I spoke them in English, then repeated in Italian for their benefit. "I am my own man. I do not need my father's guidance to choose a bride." To Allie, I spoke more softly, "I have chosen you. There is no other woman for me, for as long as live."

My grandfather's voice cut through the tension, "Dio li fa e poi li accopia." *God makes them, then joins them.* I was uncertain he meant well by that because it was commonly reserved for ill-fated couples. But the tension broke with laughter, and there were toasts to our union.

In the furor, Dianora's cousin, Leandro, leaned over her chair, whispered in her ear, then disappeared.

Much later, I snuck Allie up the back stairs so we could retire. As I stepped into the foyer, Leandro rushed from the shadows. But his knife wasn't aimed at me, he targeted Allie.

When I promised to protect her with my life, I meant it. His arm swept out as I shoved her behind me. It left me vulnerable, but his strike swung wide, still on target for Allie. I blocked the initial thrust and tied up his arm. If this were Ringo, he'd drop the knife into his other hand and I'd have left my back exposed. But Leandro was an amateur. The blow I'd braced for didn't come.

Another shadow rushed forward. I lost ground quickly as Leandro panicked.

As Loppa crashed into us, a sharp searing pain shot from my wound, and I crumbled to the ground. Luckily, Loppa was almost the same size as Dianora's hulking cousin, and he was faster. He broke our attacker's hold almost immediately. Leandro, sensing the odds had shifted drastically, ran toward the main stairs and slid down the rail with Loppa hot on his heels.

It had only been seconds, and I was spent. My breaths were jagged and raw. Between the stars in my vision, Allie stirred.

"Are you okay?" I asked.

She groaned a little, but rallied. "I'm fine, just…jostled. Oh my God, are you hurt?" She scrambled to my side and checked me for injury. Her frantic motions stilled as her hand touched the patch of blood soaking into my shirt. "*Damn* it. I think there's a small wound dehiscence on this end. Tell me that doctor left his suture kit."

"I don't know."

"Fuck!" She pressed harder against my injury. "Where's Loppa?"

She'd just finished cursing again when he stomped up the stairs. "I lost him, boss."

"Check on Don Manca." I gritted out.

"He is well, I was in his room when I heard the struggle."

"Is there anything I can use to stitch him up again?" Allie held my wound with one hand and unbuttoned my shirt with the other.

"The doctor left supplies."

"Okay, I need somewhere…not here." Her fingers were gentle against my chest. "Can you move without pulling anything else loose? I'm going to have you use your shirt to hold things in place until I can see better." She turned away from me. "Loppa, are you okay to pick him up?"

"Yes, Signora Valentini."

"On three."

We ended up in our suite. Allie checked the wound, cleaned the area and checked for damage. She chose to add what she referred to as a "zipper" to close the end that had torn open.

As she worked, my grandfather peered over her shoulder. His eyes met mine. The corner of his mouth curved upward. Then he shocked the hell out of me.

"Signora Allie, would you like to learn a language that witch and her soon-to-be-dead cousin will never know?"

Allie paused. "Depends. Is he going to stay alive long enough for me to get the first lesson?"

Don Manca laughed long and hard at that. "With your help, I'm certain he will. First lesson, I am, Aiaiu. Grandfather. When you are around family, this family, you will call me that. 'Nonno' if there are people who aren't in this circle, sì?" He paused as Allie blushed. When he spoke again, he raised his voice. "That includes nosy fathers who stand behind doorways."

My father stepped into the open. "How is he doing?"

"No thanks to you, he lives," Don Manca said.

"I was trying to stop the animosity between our families." Father fired back.

Allie nervously packed the kit she'd disassembled for my care. I caught her hand so she wouldn't flee. "Wait. Please?"

Grandfather continued berating my father. *"By selling him like a cow? Now he's hunted because you meddled."*

"Aiaiu," I cautioned him to speak kinder to my father. Logistically, it had been a sound tactic. But he should have asked me before making arrangements. "Allie, I need to speak to them about things you shouldn't know. It is for your safety that I can't include you. I promise I will not talk *around* you, or *about* you."

She nodded, but tugged her hand away. Its loss left me wanting.

I quickly laid out the problems I'd found. *"Adelmo turned down an offer of money to bail him out. He wanted his operation in the States only and wished for his family to leave him out of the global issues. But his father was not in agreement. His stipulation was for Dianora to marry someone from one of the leading families. Then she could manage her assets through proxy if she wanted, but not as an heir to the company.*

"Adelmo thought his father was right to marry her into another family to protect her share. I don't think she or her father knows that. But also, I don't think either of them know their father is making bad decisions for both of them.

"I spoke with Edward in Las Vegas. Father, you remember him, the real estate investor you were so keen to work with last year?"

"I remember."

"He gave me information that Don Conti has sold five family estates in the last year. His bank in Cyprus owes over 120 million in fines. The noose is tightening on him."

Don Manca's face turned grim. *"When was this fine?"*

"September of last year," I said.

"That's eight of our compatriot's targeted." He fixed his gaze on my father. *"And you? Any nooses?"*

"None. I know the laws."

"Let's hope you know the laws," Grandfather sniped back.

My father's tone sharpened. *"If you and your family weren't always killing everyone, I wouldn't be in the crosshairs at all. If anyone has a noose around their neck, it is you."*

Grandfather frowned. *"He still blames me for your mother's death."*

The tendons in Father's neck tightened and stood out, but otherwise, he remained calm. *"I know you didn't plant that bomb. But your enemies did."*

"And you court them. Dangle my grandson out as bait for them to devour whole."

I quickly switched back to English. "Enough! I've said my part." I studied my wife who had moved to the far side of the room to study the wallpaper. "Allie, I am so grateful you're with me. Very grateful."

She studied my father and grandfather before coming closer. "I think you both need to let him rest."

Grandfather kissed her cheek before he exited.

My father lingered. He studied the lattice of tiny plastic zip ties now holding my wound together. He turned to Allie. "You did this?"

"Yes. It's a becoming common practice for dogs. There's talk of using it on horses soon. But for people, it is quite common. You'll note I couldn't use it on the smaller section of the wound where the knife cut upward on its way out. But that part is healing well on its own."

Father turned white.

Allie noticed and pulled a chair behind him. He sat, almost bonelessly.

"Twice. You were almost killed twice."

He spoke English for Allie's sake. But I wasn't going to be as kind and switched so only my father could understand. *"Tonight, I wasn't the target. My wife was."*

His eyes met mine. In their depths was fear and a grief he'd never gotten over. I was a bit too young to understand it all at the time, but the way he shut down after she died hurt me harder than losing my mother did. Now I finally understood how he survived. I felt it in my heart. I'd been the cold, calculating shadow of my father for so long, just a few short days with Allie opened a door I barely remembered.

If my father loved my mother half as much, and if she had brought half as much light to his world, losing her must have broken him. As losing Allie would likely break me.

I was only beginning to know her and was already drowning.

12

ALLIE

Despite Mario's promise not to talk about me, or around me, the hushed whispers with his guards and Aiaiu were just that. It's amazing how much body language plays a part in communication. The glances, the sudden silences when I entered a room told a story that was plain. I'd stepped in it. But no one would explain it to me.

"You can't stand near the window." Loppa's hand barred me from peering out the top floor's suite window.

"Why?"

He glanced toward Don Manca's room as if searching for guidance from his boss. However, both Aiaiu and Mario were deep in discussion with his father. Something had changed and those three were thick as thieves lately.

"Tell me, Loppa. Did I imagine that knife aimed at me?"

He paled. "We are taking care of that."

Ah. As in taking care of *permanently*. Something I really

didn't need to know. I'd not only made a huge error trusting Mario, but also in coming to Italy. These men made my grandfather look like…well, an accountant.

In frustration, I tried calling my sister, again. She hadn't answered any of my calls since that odd conversation where she'd hung up on me. I needed her now. She'd tell me exactly what she thought. Or worse, take on an obviously established crime organization's whole family to spring me from this luxury prison. Of course, the conversation could go in the opposite direction with Ellie telling me to "go for it" and live a little. But this wasn't living. It was hiding— which didn't sit well with Mario.

That was plain.

He was cranky, nervous, irritable, and short. Not with me, but with everyone else, even his grandfather.

From the tight way Loppa tensed his proverbial butthole, I'd guess not many spoke to Don Manca that way.

I dug out my headphones and doubled down on learning Italian from the language app on my phone.

"The villa is safest." Don Manca issued his opinion like an order.

"It is —" Was that word "isolated?"

"Perhaps the island?" His father suggested.

I scrambled to find the auto translator which could display the speech in text on my screen.

"It is too far to travel." Mario used the same authoritative tone his grandfather had.

Loppa reached across my line of vision and pulled the phone from my hands. His frown held a hint of amusement, but he shook his head at me anyway.

Busted. "You'd do the same thing," I told him.

"You'll learn the language faster by hearing it and understanding it, not translating it."

My glare was a language of its own. One that made Loppa shift uncomfortably.

"They are making travel plans, we can't stay in Milan."

"You'd think a member of government would have better security," I muttered.

"His team are amateurs." Loppa's smug chin shifted higher into the air. "Come, I think you need a break."

He led me to a space two floors down. Firenze lounged on a long couch while a few of Don Valentini's guards monitored the security feeds in an adjacent room.

"I thought we were going outside." It came out as a pout.

"Not an option. You are homesick. Pick a movie." Loppa handed me the remote for the television and with it, my phone.

I wasn't homesick, was I? I glanced at my phone to see if Ellie had called.

Damn. He nailed my problem with deadly accuracy. I picked up the remote determined to not blush beet red.

As I scrolled through the thumbnails, a familiar mask stood out. I paused on it. I'd never actually seen the opera or the movie. *Perhaps?*

"Loppa, do you like opera?"

"Bella signora, opera is in the life blood here."

Good. I tapped play.

Loppa was the armchair-commentator type movie watcher. Firenze was the silent observer. I was somewhere between and Loppa switched to English for most of his criticism.

"This is not an opera."

"The music, ugh…repetitive."

"Their swords are dull."

But about half-way through both Firenze and Loppa shifted to the edge of their seats.

"That is ridiculous! Use a garrote you idiot."

Firenze's softer voice commented, and I couldn't make out what he said.

"What is wrong with that?"

Loppa pulled the remote from my hand and jogged the scene to the beginning. "Okay. She tells him to keep his hand at the level of his eyes. Good."

Firenze held up his hand to illustrate.

"But, a noose? Please. You can't conceal it; you can't loop it quickly enough. And it is much harder to push a garrote away. One must turn into the pull."

"Sorry?"

"Let's demonstrate," Firenze offered.

He stood, just like the love interest did.

"My hand is here."

Loppa stood behind him and brought out a very real, very wicked-looking cord.

"Is that real?"

"Eh, anything is a garrote, but wire is best. It hurts more. Perhaps I should change this… Firenze?"

"Don't bother. This is a child's technique."

The sinister way Loppa grinned wasn't reassuring. He explained his move. "A *professional* would see his hand ready and pull their knife. One quick thrust through the ribs here —does the trick easily. But let's say we are not dealing with professionals. I come over his head like this." He had the wire in front of Firenze almost immediately. The edge dug into his raised wrist.

Firenze picked up the commentary. "In the movie, he catches the attempt with his arm. Good, but…" He turned his head to the side and braced his fist against his cheek. "You brace your head on the attacker's shoulder so he can't pull you off balance. As you do this, pull down on the wire. Turn your body so it is facing your attacker. See? Your arm is still trapped and using your weight against their arm, but your other arm is free. Strike."

He swung his free arm and stopped short of Loppa's nuts.

"Here. *Hard*. Hit harder than you think you can, as many times as you can. Understand? Five times harder. Strike fast. You cannot hit hard enough." He swung his arm. Loppa turned to avoid a direct hit.

"This is practice, my friend."

Firenze grinned. "Loppa turned, but you see, he is now paying attention to where you are striking and it added slack on the cord. You can breathe." He angled his arm and pulled the garrote taut, then ducked his head through the opening to escape the noose. "You escape."

"Again."

Firenze went back to his initial position.

Loppa came up behind him. "This will be the professional attack, if they have no knife, or need the kill to be very quiet. I will loop the cord, cross my hands, turn to pull him off his feet."

Similar to before, Loppa swept his arms over Firenze's head but he crossed his right hand over his left, making the noose tighter than before. "A professional crosses the wire, see? Then twists, so."

Firenze turned, slapped Loppa's leg, then tapped his fists into Loppa's chest, chin, and ended with a strike to the jaw with his open palm. "The trick is to always turn to face the attacker as quickly as possible, and keep your feet under you. You cannot lose your balance. If you do, get as close to the attacker as possible for the turn. Let's show her without the hand up."

Loppa moved behind him again, and this time Firenze didn't have his hand up.

"A moment." Loppa undid his belt and slipped the garrote into a sleeve. "I'll hurt him less this way," he told me.

This time their moves were so fast I could barely see what happened. Loppa twisted and they scrambled several steps as Firenze turned toward him, keeping one hand on the belt and his feet scrambling with the motion of the pull. He hit Loppa and they went down to the ground. A vase on a nearby table became unbalanced and tilted sharply to the edge. I jumped up and caught it in time to save it.

Loppa and Firenze were on the carpet grinning up at me.

"See?" Loppa said. "Amateurs would use something so obvious." He pointed at the movie.

"Your turn." Firenze suggested.

"Oh, no."

"You need to know this. Like he said, it is a child's lesson." Loppa pointed at the spot where Firenze stood before.

"Go easy on me."

"I will."

After the third instruction, he quickened the pace, and I misread his attack, fell backward into Loppa, lost my footing, and practically choked myself on the belt he used.

"That'll leave a bruise," Firenze commented. "You need to be more careful with your nephew's bride."

"Do you think her attackers will be careful?"

Before they could argue more, Mario stepped into the room. "What are you doing?!"

From my vantage point on the carpet, I was able to see both Loppa and Firenze freeze in place. The guilty grimaces on their faces were easy to read.

I brushed my knees off, preparing to stand. "We were watching your movie."

"*My* movie?"

The screen was still paused at the point Loppa stopped it. The phantom in the mask frozen in place, a rope in his hands.

Mario shifted his eyes from the screen to me. "You see me as a villain?"

"No." Unfortunately, I didn't sound as certain as I felt. Maybe I wasn't certain at this point. There were similarities. For instance, I wasn't free to leave. From Firenze to Don Manca, they truly believed it was for my safety, but I wasn't buying it anymore.

"Cara."

I lifted my eyebrow. Sure, I knew the word meant heart or beloved or something like that, and I could tell by Mario's tone he was using it as a term of endearment, but were we there yet?

He held out his hand.

I let him help me up.

No sooner than I was on my feet, he turned my chin from one angle to the other, checking the damage to my neck. The grim frown and the tightness of his jaw were an instant clue to the emotions running through his thoughts.

"Loppa?" Mario spoke his name without shifting his gaze away from me.

"Nephew."

Mario paused. Loppa practically growled the word.

"I didn't know he was your uncle."

"He is Don Manca's third son. Just a few years older than my mother."

I stared at his eyes to tell him to calm down and that I was unharmed. Embarrassed, sure. But then again, as Loppa repeatedly stated, I knew less than a child. But if they taught this technique to their children, that meant Mario must have learned in a similar manner. "I'm not hurt."

His finger traced across my neck. It traveled along the path that had hurt the worst, but the sting was almost gone. His fingertip actually tickled, and I flinched.

"Not hurt?"

"That tickles."

His frown cleared, and a small smile replaced it. His eyes

moved to lock onto mine. And once again he traced along my neck.

I fought the urge to flinch away again. But he hit the softer skin behind my ear and I twisted to avoid further torment.

"Firenze will instruct her until she's better acclimated to the lifestyle. He is my second cousin, and not so bloodthirsty."

Silence greeted Mario's order. He turned to scrutinize Loppa. "Are we clear?"

His uncle remained silent for a short time longer. "I will cover the *non*-contact safety training. For example, entering and exiting buildings and vehicles."

Mario nodded. "That will be acceptable."

He glanced at the screen again. "How is the movie?"

"Not nearly as good as the wedding was," I said.

Mario grinned. "We have time before we leave. Shall we?" He took my hand and led me to the couch.

Loppa backtracked the movie once more as I caught Mario up on the plot up to that point.

We settled in, holding hands and quiet as Loppa continued his commentary. I forgot about watching the movie, and instead studied the light play across Mario's face. He was more handsome today than ever. But I could still remember the way the mask obscured his face, and gave him a sinister air.

Yes, he was a villain in some ways. His family definitely had their sketchy qualities. His father was almost a caricature of polished political power. His grandfather was an enigma. Kind, with a wicked sense of humor, and just enough shadows in his eyes that you knew he wasn't as wholesome as he seemed.

Loppa could easily be cast into the role of villain, but I liked him best because he was supremely honest even when he hid things from me.

Firenze was competent.

Mario was all of that rolled into one man. Villain, enigma, polished, competent, and most of all, a gentleman.

Yet lurking underneath there were qualities that made my insides squirm, and my heart race. I could imagine him healthy and unleashed. Then he'd be a force of nature.

But more than all of that, he was my hero…my husband.

13

MARIO

*Non c'è niente oltre te. — There is nothing
beyond you.*

The familiar scents of dry wood, aged stone, and the ever-present tang of ocean air pleased my senses as I breathed in the crisp morning air.

Last night's meal was tense. Much of the conversation with my father and grandfather centered around the price on my head and the last few days. A few times they'd mention Allie, who pretended to ignore the conversation. But with her quick mind, she understood far more than she could translate.

And astute as she was, she insisted we retire immediately after a late meal and our even later hasty travel to my grandfather's villa on the coast between Zoagli and Chiavari. The first and last thing she did was check my damaged side and order rest.

Luckily, the wound stayed closed despite everyone's best efforts to maim me. And the solid sleep I got did wonders. When I stretched to greet the sun, my wound didn't pinch. It only felt tight.

Allie rolled to her side so she could blink the sleep out of her eyes and stare at my nakedness.

"Good morning, my beautiful wife."

"You look… good." Her eyes dipped to my semi-hard cock and her cheeks flushed pink.

I smiled. I felt good. Strong for the first time in possibly three days. Grounded instead of hunted. And best of all, I had the most beautiful of women captive in my soft, warm bed. I shut the cold out and rejoined her.

"And you look beautiful," I said as I crawled onto the bed to join her.

"My hair is a mess, and I have no makeup on. You're delusional."

"No. I'm quite sane." I tugged on one of her twisted blonde locks in order to tease her. "*Kiss me.*"

"You're going to strain yourself again."

"Only in the best ways." I leaned against her and stole a kiss.

"Your skin is cold." She pushed against my shirtless chest.

"Perhaps you can warm it up?" I slipped under the heavy quilt.

A sly smile worked across her face. "You must be feeling a lot better."

I nibbled on the curve of her ear where she was ticklish. The time for talk was over.

She dodged my teeth the second time I tried, but moved closer to me instead of away. Her hands caressed my skin. I returned the favor by sweeping my palms down the delicate negligee she wore.

"Another of your sister's indulgences?" I had been in too much pain recently to notice.

"Maybe?"

I snuck a glance at the lace covering her. The fine camisole was transparent. The virginal white pattern of roses and interlocking leaves, exposed her breasts indecently with tantalizing glimpses of the peachy rose surrounding her peaked nipples. I licked one tip to taste her skin.

She sucked air in through her teeth.

I opened my mouth wider and flattened my tongue against the lace, letting it soak the fabric until it the fibers turned translucent. Then I closed my mouth over her breast.

Her fingers tightened in my hair. "Mario." The slight stutter of her breath betrayed her. I repeated my actions on the other side, then ran my teeth on the protruding nipple.

But the lace was in the way. I wanted nothing between us.

I lifted up to take in the outfit. The lace continued all the way to the hem. The sheerness of the fabric leaving little to the imagination.

The matching panties were just as sheer. "*Wife*," I growled.

"You like?"

"I want you naked."

She pretended to pout. "This is the only pretty

nightgown I've *ever* worn, and he doesn't like it." She chanced a glance at me through her eyelashes.

"I never said I didn't like it. I said, I. Want. You. Naked." This time, the warmth dropped from my tone and was replaced by demand.

Her eyes went wider.

But she didn't move. I slipped a hand under the hem and cupped it around her breast. The fabric strained. "I might damage this. And then, you'll have to explain to your sister what happened to this beautiful garment."

She sat up, pulling the top off as quickly as she could.

That was better. I returned to the damp nipple I'd tasted. This time, it was sweet with a subtle flavor that was natural and intoxicating. And when I sucked the peak into my mouth, there was no fabric foiling my tongue. I rolled it in in my mouth, swirling around the tip, and taking it deeper until Allie gasped and arched into me. Her fingers curled into my scalp and the words spilling from her mouth slurred in ecstasy.

But I wasn't done. The other side needed as much attention if not more because it had been forgotten for too long.

"Mario. Please?" *Please-please-please more.* I heard her begging in my head as much as through my ears.

The lace between her legs was wet. My fingertips ran across the panel searching for the forbidden and once again, was denied access.

Screw that. I gripped the tiny bands holding the garment in place.

"Don't. Don't tear it, please?"

A guttural sound emanated from my chest. I didn't slide the panties off gently, but they remained intact when I tossed them as far as I could from the bed.

It was only me and my wife now.

She stroked my cock timidly. I curled my hand over hers and tugged it down the length the way I liked it.

Her eyes met mine.

I nodded and led her actions. She mimicked them, getting bolder with each stroke. I groaned out loud. Much more of that, and I'd embarrass myself.

With effort, I pulled free and slid down her body until my mouth aligned with her beautiful pussy. It tasted like perfection. Slick and ready, but not thoroughly debauched. *Yet.*

I dragged the tip of my tongue through the valleys and around the tiny crown of her clit. With each gasp and jolt, I learned her weaknesses and the magical combination of pressure and circling that fluttered her eyelids shut, or caught her breath.

She was complex, my bride. A tasty puzzle I longed to unravel, savor, and enjoy many times over.

Her cry of satisfaction bounced off the low farmhouse ceiling and the stucco walls. With one final sweep of my tongue, I abandoned her for a moment to reach for a condom.

But I wasn't at home, nor in a hotel I'd thoroughly planned in advance to seduce her in. And knew I'd come up empty in the sterile nightstand placed for aesthetics rather than function.

"Allie?"

Her unfocused eyes met mine.

I wanted this woman. She could be bound to me forever, if only I was as conniving as my father. "I don't have a condom," I confessed.

"Oh! My sister packed dozens in her bag, hang on." She scrambled out of bed and returned quickly with a box.

I took it from her and retrieved a foil-wrapped packet from inside but hesitated.

Our eyes met. She was on her knees, facing me.

This was my *wife*.

Mine. To have, hold, cherish, protect, and treasure. "Mi Amore…"

"I know that one." Her lips met mine. When our kiss broke, she held my face in her hands. "Do *not* strain yourself."

"I won't." I lied. Despite my best intentions, I couldn't help but don protection and lift her with the intent of getting her on her back as soon as humanly possible.

Her mumbled words against my lips were ignored as I slid inside. The warmth of the welcome sent a shock wave from my scalp to my toes and I clung to her for a moment to savor the bliss.

"*My wife, my love, my life. I will be your servant always.*" With effort, I backed out, leaving only the tip of my cock notched in her cunt, then slowly pressed my way inward until I seated against her again. "*I'm undone by you.*"

She blinked, not understanding my words. "Mario…" her mouth worked, trying to voice silent desires.

"Say you want this." I was clear, direct. Being careful to get her full permission.

"I want you. It's such a bad idea, but I do. I can't not want you."

The words were balm to my heart. I poured myself into each thrust, each foreign utterance of my joy. The whispers of my desires confessed into her untrained ear. Was it wrong to yearn for a future where she'd understand? Would we be blessed with the years it would take for her to understand the language of my heart?

I knew some of it sank in because her eyes were wide-open, trusting, and reflecting the passion I felt. "My love," I spoke in English so she'd understand me.

"You're a dream. A fantasy I didn't know I had. Please?"

"Non c'è niente oltre te." I could see nothing in my life without her. My passion flared and I forgot gentility. Our bodies danced irresistibly, unerringly, and most importantly, honestly. My walls were gone, and she was the only thing I knew in that moment.

Her shuddering orgasm pulsed around me. It undid me. I came. The rush of pleasing her released the final bonds of control.

And with the finality, joy filled my heart.

I possessed a heart. The marvel of it made me pause as I caught my breath.

Allie's hand stroked down my spine. "Are you okay?" She was as breathless as I was.

In that last fragment of honesty, I felt a twinge at my side. "I tried."

"And?"

How to say it? "I did not damage myself."

Her face crumbled a little. "Slow movements. Please?"

"For you, anything."

Yet it wasn't enough. I ended up on my back, drained and remembering a betrayal that shouldn't have happened. My hand held the bandage in place.

"Do I dare look?" she asked.

"No." I sighed.

She brushed away a curl of hair that clung to my forehead. The cool air of the ocean replaced it and calmed me. "I'm going to check."

"You can't help it, can you?"

Her expression spoke for her. She curled into the same non-threatening kneel she'd adopted on the plane. The silence, while comforting in ways I didn't understand also put a barrier between us. And that would not do. She needed to know that in everything, she was perfection.

"Your compassion toward wounded creatures doesn't change the fact that I am hopelessly in love with you. Not because you care for me when I'm like this, but because I've found my heart. You've found my heart."

"Oh, Mario, I—"

A knock on the door interrupted what she was going to say. Despite my state of undress and the sacredness of this moment, I had to answer it. And preferably without exposing my lovely bride to scrutiny.

I rolled out of bed and dragged a robe off the chair. Allie scrambled to cover herself up to her chin with the comforter. I answered the door. Firenze was behind it, attempting to look anywhere but inside the room. In rapid-fire words he summarized the situation.

"Ringo has surfaced. He is at the cliff house. There's a woman with him."

I lowered my volume. *"Does this woman look like my wife?"*

"Sì, Don Valentini."

"Do not take him there, especially in front of the woman. He'll come to us. Prepare. I want him alive."

"Mario?" Allie called from the bed.

I thanked Firenze for his warning and rejoined my wife.

"Is everything okay?"

"It is fine. Have you heard from your sister lately?"

Allie frowned. "No. I'm worried about her."

"There may have been progress on that front."

"Really? Did you find her? Is she okay? Can I see her?" She scrambled out of bed and began to grab lingerie from her sister's suitcase. She picked a bright blue pairing that reminded me of spring flowers.

"Allie, it was only a sighting. They wanted me to know."

Her shoulders deflated. "Oh. Did they say where she was?"

I smiled. "Did your itinerary include Pisa?"

It only took a moment for her to recall the plans she'd memorized. "No, we opted out of it because of the travel and Cinque Terra being off-season, and…She's there?"

"Perhaps."

Allie's hope slowly drained from her face.

"What is wrong, my love?"

"She hasn't even tried to call me."

Ah. In a small way, I understood her disappointment. Ringo hadn't made contact, either. Of course, I expected him not to, except in the most violent of ways, but that didn't change my disappointment.

"She will call." She'd better. Or else I'd send Firenze and Loppa, and perhaps a dozen more men with them to extract her from my very dead friend's clutches.

14

ALLIE

The terrace was lovely, but a bit chilly. The view faced west toward the sea. The water was choppy and very few boats braved the rough water. But early almond blooms scented the air, and there were fresh roses in the vases gracing the side tables.

Mario placed me nearest the house, with a slightly obstructed view of the water. I didn't mind. I was watching him. He was moving much easier today. No flinching, no protective covering of the wound site, except when he sat. That was good.

"No fever?"

He smiled and continued spreading a soft cheese on the bread in his hand. "None. No pain, except when I move certain ways, which you'd correct me for, so I don't. And the site is…guarded well by your little plastic fortress."

I shook my head. He was such a tough nut. But I was cracking him. His smile was easy. The moments when he'd glance up and his breath caught were my favorite. And this home? I could live here. It was beautiful. Rustic, rural enough to have gardens and grapevines, but strategically set into a steeply terraced hillside that must have been dug out centuries ago.

"How old is that city?" I pointed at the collection of houses below us.

He craned his head to look. "I would guess four centuries. It came with the fish."

"Do you fish?"

He nodded. A small smile of memory lifted one side higher than the other. "We have a boat… I have a boat."

Ringo. Every once in a while, Mario would slip up and refer to his friend as a part of him. He must be grieving the loss of friendship and worrying. Much like I was worrying about Ellie.

Perhaps thinking of her made me check my phone. Or maybe it was that odd quirk of twins. No matter the distance, sometimes we thought on the same wavelength. My phone lit up with a strange number. I hesitated to answer it at the breakfast table.

Mario however, didn't mind. He circled his fingers in the air to let me know I should proceed.

"Allie?" My sister's voice sounded clearer than I would have expected.

"Ellie, where are you?"

"I'm going to ask you the same damn thing. I went to Venice then Milan, and—"

"What happened to your phone?"

"Oh, that. It's long-ass story. I guess you could say I

dropped it in the canal, but more like it got knocked out of my hand and… well, that's not all of it, but enough."

"I'm sorry."

"Don't worry about it. Your notes helped a little. Ringo helped more. He's the one who got me this phone."

"Ringo?" I asked. My eyes shot to Mario.

Suspiciously, he was not shocked by the news. How many men were named Ringo? My guess would be not many. And certainly not enough to overcome the massive odds against my twin sister hooking up with my husband's… attempted murderer? Best friend?

Oh *hell*. That wasn't coincidental at all. "You knew?"

Mario's eyebrow lifted slightly. Behind him, Loppa studied the landscape, or at least pretended to in order to avoid my sharp glare.

"I knew what?" Ellie asked.

"Where are you now?" And more importantly, was she with him?

"Oh, I'm on this little hiking trail near some coastal town. I don't know what it's called, but it's pretty. We boated over from Portofino this morning."

"We?"

"Ringo and I. Babe, what are you doing?"

The latter half of her conversation must have been directed at Ringo. I quickly covered the end of my phone with my hand to muffle my voice. "She's with *him*, Ringo."

"Who are you talking to, Allie?" Ellie asked.

"My husband."

"Whoa. Wait a minute, you're serious? You really married someone you just met? You can't do that."

"Why not? How long did you know Johnny Pornstash, a month?"

"It's Porciello, and I didn't marry him, so you've already slid down that slippery slope of matrimony, my little black teapot twinsie."

I opened my mouth to bitch her out but got interrupted.

"Would you look at that?"

"What?" I asked Ellie.

"I can see you. You're on a terrace with a couple of bruisers walking around the edges, and holy shit, is that *It's-a-me-Mar-ee-oh*?"

"You can see me?" I stood up and started to walk to the edge, but Mario jumped out of his seat and got in front of me."

Then the damnedest thing happened. Or should I say, a bunch of damned things happened.

"Ringo, what the hell?" Ellie's voice rang in my ear as the ceramic pot near my head splintered and the crack of a bullet ricocheted off the pot into the tiled floor at our feet. Mario pushed me down and dragged me under the table.

Loppa and Firenze sprung into motion, Loppa landing on top of Mario, who was on top of me, and Firenze drawing a weapon to shoot at whoever was shooting at us.

I still had the phone in hand, and could hear my sister bitching up a storm at Ringo. "Who in the fuck are you shooting at?"

"He's shooting at us," I relayed to Mario. Another volley of shots peppered against the roof. One smacked into the wall near us and a chunk of masonry broke away at high speed. It hit Loppa in the shoulder and a piece of it cut his cheekbone too close to his eyes for me to do anything but scream.

Mario rolled off me, a gun in hand, his eyes trained on the hillside.

Before I could blink, he'd sprinted to the wall, braced a shoulder on it and sent two rapid-fire shots up the slope.

Another shot echoed against the hills and I reached out to Mario, hoping it wasn't too late to hold him, or touch his skin, or perhaps even simply tell him how damn much he'd begun to mean to me.

But the rifle sound that answered came from almost directly equal with our terrace on the hillside.

"Allie?" Ellie screamed into the phone.

"I'm okay."

"He shot him. I don't believe it. He shot him!" My sister was rapidly becoming hysterical.

"Who did he shoot?" Mario and a bleeding Loppa peered over the wall. Firenze had already sprinted off to climb the terraces upward.

"I don't know, but he shot him." Ellie was sobbing now.

A man's voice sounded harsh in my ear. "Is Valentine near you?"

"What?"

"Valentine. Tell him to get his head down."

I didn't know what to do, or who this man was. Was it Ringo?

"Allie? Your husband is a sitting fucking duck where he is. Give him the fucking phone right now. Or better yet, tell him this: 'That's two.'"

Mario was about to move. "Mario?"

"Cara mia, stay here."

"No. Ringo says, 'That's two.'"

He looked at me strangely. For a heartbeat, I saw someone completely different staring out from my husband's eyes. This man was cold, calculating, deadly. Definitely not the warm, caring man I'd slept with. A slither of fear tickled my spine right between my shoulder blades.

"Honey? He says you need to get your head down."

Mario quickly crouched. "Where is he?"

"Where are you?" I could still hear my sister swearing in the background.

"On the south trail coming up from the beach, not the boat landing."

I relayed that to Mario. He quickly got on his phone to Firenze and directed him to intercept Ringo. Firenze fired something back and an exchange of rapid Italian bounced between them.

Mario directed a question to me, "Ringo is on that call?"

I nodded.

Loppa cried out, "If you don't kill him now, I will!"

"Quiet." Mario stared at me and then glanced at the holes in the canopy above us.

"Boss?" Loppa tried again.

Mario ignored him. "Allie? Hold out the phone and put it on speaker, but do not come to me, understand?"

I nodded and stretched my arm to its full length and tried not to shiver too much as the conversation continued between Mario, Firenze, Ringo, and an irate Loppa, who'd crawled closer to me.

Blood trailed from his cheek, and he'd pressed a

handkerchief to it, but his shoulder was also bleeding. I snatched one of the cloth napkins from the table and pressed it against that wound.

Eventually, Mario crawled to me and took the phone from my hand so I could tend to Loppa without impediment. Both wounds were superficial. The shoulder took the brunt of the force, but bled less thanks to the heavy coat he'd worn. His cheek only needed a couple of butterfly bandages.

However, he had difficulty raising his arm. I suggested he should get it examined, but he ignored me as Firenze escorted Ringo and my sister to Mario's doorstep.

Ellie looked shell-shocked. Her skin was too pale even though she'd stopped screaming for now. In fact, she was uncharacteristically quiet.

We'd moved inside, with Firenze calling for reinforcements and more guards to sweep the slope. I handed Ellie a glass of orange juice I'd salvaged from the terrace, against orders, but she needed the sugar. Then I wrapped a blanket around her.

"Why are you covered in blood?" Her voice wobbled, but luckily she stayed conscious.

I looked down. This morning's pretty ivory and rose dress was ruined. I'd skinned a knee, and Loppa's blood had stained the bodice. "It's Loppa's." I swept a coat off a nearby chair to cover it so she wouldn't pass out.

"The big guy with no neck?" she clarified.

"He's a teddy bear."

"I am not." Loppa passed through the house carrying a long rifle.

"Where are they getting these guns? Italy is really strict about it."

I glanced at my sister. Her color was finally returning. Also, her characteristic chattiness was slowly resurfacing. "How do you know about their gun laws?"

"Pornstash."

"I can't believe you're calling him that."

Her cheek flinched slightly. "You were right."

As much as I used to relish that sentence falling from her lips, I had a feeling I'd been *very* wrong lately. Ellie's comment about guns was only one reason.

"Johnny's a bad guy." Although she was recovering, her blank stare betrayed her state of shock.

The hustle of men carrying guns in and out of the house was the only noise for a long time.

Unspoken was a judgment on the men surrounding us. Instead, she finally started with "So… you're married?"

"I should have waited, right? Maybe get your lawyer to check him out?" I braced for her 'What were you thinking' tirade.

But it didn't come.

Ellie stared out the window. Through it, I could see the profile of the man she'd been with. He was that same good-looking rogue who'd vowed to kill Mario for stealing my ride share. Yet, I knew those bullets bouncing off the patio came from the slope above, not the paths from the ocean. But I had to be sure. "You hiked up the hill?"

"Oh my fucking God, yes. That was a killer. You were right about the tourist shoes, too. Damn you."

"How far up the slope were you?"

"It felt like miles, but probably only halfway up. My thighs are killing me. How did you get in this mess, Allie?"

"I got married."

Ellie's face soured. "That's not like you at all."

No, it wasn't. Nothing had been like me since walking into that wedding chapel.

"Mom and Dad were watching the live feed," I mused.

Ellie bit her lip. She did that when she didn't want to admit she was at fault for something.

"They would have loved your wedding to that…man. Probably not the divorce, but…"

"Are you going to divorce him?" Her eyes nudged toward the slope where Mario and his men hunted down whoever had been shooting at us.

That was a good question. I should. I should run for the hills, tuck tail, and fly home. I should do a lot of things. But mainly, I didn't want to. Call me foolish, or just plain brainwashed, but I liked the people around Mario.

Well, maybe not his father, or that witch, Dianora, or her cousin. And definitely not whoever was shooting at him. And the jury was still a month or more out on Ringo because he'd hurt his best friend. But overall, these people were… intense, protective, warm, humble… I smiled. They were a family. I wanted that. Probably since Mom and Dad fled to Arizona.

But I should divorce him. It would be the smart thing to do. Mario was a very dangerous man.

My sister asked the most important question of all. One I'd carefully avoided. "You're in love with him, aren't you?"

Yes. I was.

15

MARIO

We found the body of a man near the top of the hill. Firenze spotted the muzzle flash during the exchange and had finally located where he had landed inside a small grove of scrubby strawberry trees.

He'd been dead before he finished falling.

And the bullet hole between his eyes wasn't from one of my men's guns.

No, this had Ringo's signature all over it. *"Dispose of this."*

Firenze nodded and picked two men to carry the corpse away. Meanwhile Loppa complained. Maybe it was the pain, or the close call. But it was likely because I'd insisted on joining the search.

I had to. I couldn't face Ringo without the murderous urge to destroy him eating at my chest.

Too soon, Loppa and I returned to the scene of our

ruined breakfast and the dotted blood splotches that proved one of my men paid a price to protect me.

That wasn't how it was supposed to be.

The urge to kill Ringo was strong. "You bastard."

"That's the way my father made me," he joked. I'd heard it often.

"You brought this to my door."

"I did no such thing," Ringo fired back. Then he pointed at the slope we'd just returned from. "And that? What did you find up there?"

"A body," Loppa growled

Ringo grinned. "That's two, Mario… Damn it, think!"

"About what? You stabbed me."

"It was habit! How many times have we sparred like that? How many times do I have to tell you to trap the arm before it comes across the body? You're still making that mistake. You're just lucky I wasn't *really* trying to kill you."

Allie rushed out. I grabbed her and pulled her under the overhang. Even though we'd swept the hillside, that didn't mean it was safe.

"Are you okay? Really okay?" She was careful not to touch my wounded side, but searched my eyes for the truth.

"I'm fine."

Ringo kept ranting. "And this bullshit with you sitting in the open. Fucking paint a goddamn sign on your back or something!"

Ellie followed her sister onto the terrace.

No fewer than three people shouted, including Ringo. "Get inside."

"No. I thought—"

It was clear she was confused. Worse? Emotionally attached to Ringo. That bastard likely seduced my wife's sister. I rounded on him. "You've delivered the girl. Leave."

"No can do. I control your marker and figured out a way to clear you."

"What?" Allie stepped in front of me, as if to protect me. I gathered her under an arm to tug her into my shadow.

"Show him, Ellie," Ringo prompted.

"I don't fucking have to show him anything. And you… y-you shot someone."

Like it mattered to Ringo. He'd lord that kill over my head for a year or more if we survived the day.

"The papers, Ellie. You know, about that douchebag Pornstach."

"You told *him* the nickname?" Allie asked her sister.

"It slipped out, I couldn't help it." Ellie shrugged and dug into her tote bag. She handed a stack of papers to Allie. "Here."

"This is your itinerary for Rome." Allie barely glanced at the pages and set them on the side table next to her. I picked them up and scanned them because the timetable summary on top caught my eye.

"Shit." Ellie dug in the tote again. "Sorry, *this* stack."

I reached across my wife to intercept the handoff. I tucked the travel information under the new pile.

There were multiple photos of Adelmo Conti's murder scene. The car he'd been driving had been t-boned in an intersection. It would have been ruled an accident except for the bullet holes in his chest and between his eyes. Messy. How anyone thought *I* did this was beyond me.

I shuffled through the pages and asked Ringo, "What am I looking at?"

"A set up, that's what."

No shit. "Why?"

"Probably because you were poking your nose in where it shouldn't." Ringo's tone was defensive. "And seriously? *Dianora*?"

I glanced at Allie. Her eyebrow arched with jealousy almost as soon as the name registered. I hurried to add, "She means nothing to me."

Unfortunately, my wife was not only beautiful, but wise. "Obviously, she's a part of this mess."

"But not your concern," I reminded her.

"Wait, who is he talking about?" Ellie butted in.

Allie's mouth tightened, as if guarding her secrets like a dragon. I would not enlighten her sister, either.

"The black widow of Tuscany," Ringo supplied.

Ellie glared at him. "Explain."

"No." My single word was a command. Ringo should not and would not discuss business in front of my bride or her twin.

Now, not only Allie's expression, but his soured.

My wife spoke up. "The other woman."

"She is not the other woman," I interjected.

Ellie interrupted. "Does that makes *my sister* the other one?"

Something in Ellie's tone gave me pause. Perhaps it was the way her fingers curled at her side.

"You stepped in that one," Ringo muttered and scratched the back of his neck nervously.

"Not at all." My denial was ignored.

Allie studied me. "I think I know what's happening here."

I hoped not. *"My love…"* I cautioned her not to betray any secrets.

"No, hear me out, maybe talking through this will help everyone figure out what the heck we're going to do next."

"Inside, maybe?" Ringo suggested.

"Yes. Inside," Loppa agreed. He'd turned a bit gray from the pain. Yet he was the last person to leave the terrace. He followed Ringo with a wary eye.

We gathered around the lightly crackling fireplace that heated the cozy living room on the lower level. Allie took the pages and spread them out across the coffee table. Their grisly nature was a contrast to the delicate china teacups that the chef filled to warm us up.

Allie started as soon as the servant retreated. "Okay. Let's lay out the timeline, please? How soon after you heard about your father's deal with Dianora did you travel to Chicago to speak with her brother?"

"The same day." I studied the occupants to gauge their reactions.

Ellie stared at Ringo. "You're a mobster?" Her voice was small.

"So's he." Ringo jabbed a finger in my direction.

Her eyes widened a little. My wife's however, did not. This was not news to her despite my best efforts to shield her from the truth. She'd adapted quickly. I admired her ability to compartmentalize. So much so, that I drew her hand to my mouth for a kiss.

Both Ringo and Ellie eyed me with suspicion. They'd taken seats on the chairs instead of the couch where Allie and I sat. Loppa pulled out a chair from the dining area and sat with his eyes on the windows behind Allie and I.

Ringo angled his chair closer to Ellie in such a way that he could cover the hill's sloping view.

Notably, Ellie moved her chair farther from him.

Undeterred, he shifted the chair again, bringing it an inch closer.

She turned her whole body away from him. Interesting. Their silent argument spoke volumes. The bastard had hurt her, or lied to her. But she wasn't running from him, yet.

Frustrated, Ellie blurted out, "I don't fucking believe this. First Johnny, now you two. What are the odds?"

"Considering who our grandfather was?" Allie pointed her question at her twin.

"You'd think the whole world was run by thugs." Ellie threw one hand out from her tightly crossed body. Even her legs were crossed.

"Thugs? That's all you think of me?"

Ringo sounded wounded, but he wasn't. That was sarcasm. I'd lived with him long enough to hear the difference.

Allie cleared her throat, interrupting what her sister was going to fire back at my nemesis… and my best friend.

In the back of my mind, I knew why he took that marker. It wasn't for the challenge like he claimed. He'd taken it as an excuse to follow me and take out any hitman stupid enough to try to kill me. Our scuffle in the parking lot was just that, a scuffle. One of many we'd had over the years.

My wife carried the conversation. "Okay, since Ellie isn't up to speed, here goes. His father is a politician."

"A.K.A. crook, no doubt," Ellie muttered.

Loppa snorted, then murmured to Firenze, "*I think both of them are smart women.*"

"What did he call me?" Ellie asked Ringo.

"Smart." Ringo's translation quieted her. She twisted to send Loppa a silently mouthed, "Thank you."

Loppa grinned.

"And he's trying to increase his hold on the… shall we say, more ingrained elements of non-political power in this country by setting up an arrangement with the Conti family."

For an outsider, she was astute.

"Arrangement? Try murder." Ringo's clarification was not welcome. I held up a hand to silence him but he was having none of it.

"The black widow of Tuscany, my friend."

Allie's skin flushed red.

Ellie's eyes bounced between the three of us. "Wait a minute. By arrangement, you mean marriage? But I thought you two…"

"Precisely." I waited for the gravity of the situation to clarify in her mind.

Her eyes narrowed on Allie. "Did you know he was a mobster when you said 'I do?'"

"We didn't know the marriage was legal."

Ellie practically screamed out her frustration. "I don't

fucking believe you. My sister, the huge planner, doesn't know that Vegas weddings are one hundred percent legit?"

Allie set the piece of paper in her hand back onto the table. It was a particularly graphic photo of the front seat of Adelmo's car. Blood streaked across the seat where one of the bullets missed hitting center mass.

"Let's start there. Why did you agree to marry someone who could do this?" She pointed directly at the blood splatter on the seat.

Ringo leaned in. "Messy as fuck."

Ellie squeaked next to him and avoided the photo pile altogether. "Like you could do better?"

He sent her a look that silenced her quickly.

She looked to Allie for guidance. "Can we go home?"

"No." Allie stood up and turned to stare out the window closest to us. I wanted to grab her and pull her away from the line of fire. Firenze was not as slow.

"Signora Valentini, step away from the window."

Loppa was on his feet, too. Allie took two steps to the left and then she pointed at Loppa's chair and ordered him to sit without saying a word.

"Why not, Allie?"

"Because we're targets now, too. Which is why we need to know how Johnny is involved," she explained.

Ellie opened and closed her mouth.

"Baby sis, what happened with Johnny? Why the sudden wedding?" Allie's tone was much quieter. Without moving, she'd created a calm space for her sister to trust her and let down her guard.

Ellie glanced at Ringo first. Interesting.

I caught his attention and lifted a brow at him. *Did you know?* I asked with that gesture.

He shook his head sharply once.

"Ellie?" my wife prompted.

"It's about the money."

"Grandfather's money?" Allie prompted.

Ellie hung her head and with that movement, her shoulders slumped. "No, mine. I won the lottery."

Allie crossed to her sister and knelt on the floor in front of her. "Talk to me."

Ellie licked her lips, nervously. "Remember when we got the first settlement? On his house in Chicago?"

Allie nodded. "I remember." She slid her hand onto Ellie's knee.

Her sister latched onto her hand like a lifeline.

"I did something stupid."

The pause after her statement was long enough Loppa and Firenze shifted around the room to gain better vantage points to watch the exterior.

"What did you do?" Allie laid another hand on her sister's death grip.

"You know how you were worried the Feds would seize it and stuffed your half into the bank? Well, I took all my money and bought scratch offs. I lost half of it. Then took the half that I didn't lose on and tried to lose it, too. Because they couldn't take it if I didn't have it, right? But I won."

Allie didn't say anything, opting instead to lightly rub her sister's hands between hers.

"And then I took half of that money and kept playing."

Allie swallowed. "I didn't even care at that point. It was going to be gone with the lawsuits so I thought, fuck it."

Allie nodded. "I put mine in an interest-bearing account and keep moving the interest to my savings so they can't touch it."

Her sister grimaced. "At that point, I was playing the numbers games. And that's when I…"

Ringo shifted his attention from the window, now fully invested with Ellie's tale.

"I won big. Not mega-millions big, but big, Allie. I bought the bar where I work, and…uh… a landscaping firm, my condo, and even a few shares of stock."

Ellie looked up to see everyone staring at her. Loppa and Firenze quickly looked away but Ringo's gaze bored into her as if he was seeing her in a different light. I didn't like it at all.

But Allie kept working her quiet magic. I recognized that move. She'd disarmed me that first night by simply offering me a glass of champagne. This time, it was tea.

Ellie took a sip and continued. "I was set for life. And I still kept playing."

Her hands were shaking.

"How?" Allie's question was my own.

"Betting."

Ah.

Ringo must have had the same revelation as I did. Gambling in general was a major source of income for the family. We'd been involved in it for so long, it was all legitimate, but if Ellie had run across some of the newer players in the game, she would likely have run into issues, if not full-blown problems.

My eyes locked with my friend.

He shook his head again, this time very carefully and slowly.

"Johnny set me up with his…friend." Ellie swallowed.

"Name," I growled. This would be solved with perhaps one phone call.

Ellie looked up to stare at me. "I paid him off."

She pulled her sister's hands in close. "Allie, I paid everyone off. But Johnny was… I mean, he knew. And I had to keep some money flowing through that so he wouldn't get—"

Her words cut off sharply. She studied the room as if frightened of all of us. Which she likely was. When she finally spoke again, her voice was barely a whisper.

"They were going to kill him, Allie. I was only trying to help."

My wife did not look as empathetic as before. In fact, if I read the expression on her face, it said she didn't give two shits whether Johnny was dead or not. "By marriage?"

"I know, I should have called it off then, but I won again. And Johnny said if we got married I'd never have to—"

"Oh for the love of—Ellie, you know *better* than this."

Allie's admonition caused her sister to move back into her defensive position. Both arms crossed tightly against her body, her legs practically double-crossed. That didn't stop her from aiming true. "Tell me again, who *actually* married a mobster? Huh?"

"Enough!" Ellie's teeth were out, and my wife didn't realize the danger she was in.

"Fuck you." Ellie whipped a middle finger at me, and shifted it to a vulgar arm gesture for punctuation on the insult.

Ringo coughed to cover a laugh.

Allie sighed. "Yes, I married a man with a dubious past." She stood and brushed at the dress she wore to smooth the wrinkles from the hem. "And he's done nothing but protect me since. Johnny didn't do that for you. I *hope* you see the difference."

Her sister looked mutinous. "At least Johnny didn't get me shot at."

Allie opened and closed her mouth. I crossed the room to wrap an arm over my wife's shoulders. "How did you obtain the pictures of this event?" I motioned toward the table between the couch and the fireplace.

"Our family lawyer," Allie supplied.

"The one I hired to follow Johnny. I thought he was cheating on me." Ellie stared at the floor.

"So, blackmail and cheating?" Allie's voice was much softer now, but held a hard edge.

"Yeah. Ya happy about that?"

"No. Worried."

Ellie straightened in her chair. Her eyes drifted from Allie to me. "What are you going to do about this?"

I gritted my teeth. It is one thing to plot murder in your mind, another to mention it out loud. "First, eliminate the price on my head. These photos prove I didn't kill Adelmo Conti."

"You sure about that?" Ellie's tone was familiar. I slid my gaze to Ringo, narrowing my eyes.

He raised his eyebrows at me. "She's got a point. Her lawyer didn't catch photos of Mr. Pornstach actually doing the deed."

"It is his car, no?" I pulled a wide angle of the accident scene from the pile. The grainy photograph had been secured from a traffic camera at the intersection. A man and an accomplice exited the car that had hit Adelmo's vehicle. "It is him in the pictures, correct?"

The close-up of Johnny standing next to Adelmo's car was too grainy to positively identify the face accurately, but it was most definitely not me. With Ellie's confirmation that she'd had Johnny followed, I was cleared.

"There's still the fact that you snubbed Don Conti's daughter."

Ringo was not helping.

"You know I'm right. Don Conti would have put a hit on your head for that alone." He held out his empty hands.

Ellie's jaw tensed. "Why did you marry my sister?"

Allie went rigid under my arm.

The unvarnished truth was terrible, and very unromantic. But everyone needed to hear this—even my bodyguards.

"I was injured."

"Fuck! You and your damned bleeding heart. Allie!"

Now it was my bride's jaw that tensed. "I wasn't getting a refund from the venue because there was a justice of the peace there forcing the ceremony through. Why?"

Ellie slumped. "That was my fault."

"What?" Both Ringo and Allie's voices rose.

They stared at Ellie with utter shock, and perhaps a bit of disgust on their expressions.

"Tell me why?" I'd taken a page out of Allie's text book and softened my tone.

Ellie glared at me. "If you must know, I thought Johnny was going to get cold feet after I showed him the prenup." Her jaw stuck out.

"A prenup?"

Ellie shifted to her sister's question. "Yeah, one that said that Johnny could touch none of my money, legal or not. And, he had to stop hanging around with those friends of his or else the wedding would be instantly annulled with only my signature needed."

Allie's tension slacked, and she wavered on her feet. I guided her back to the couch.

"What? Do you think you're the only one who can plan ahead? I protected my money and made sure he couldn't blackmail me anymore."

My wife processed that.

"Where is this prenup?" I asked.

Ellie scooted off her chair and dug into the binder of travel plans. She tugged it out and handed it over. "Did you sign a prenup, Mr. Valentini?"

I did not. My wife was entitled to my entire fortune should I die. As it should be.

This time it was Ringo sending me a glare. "He didn't. It's against the code." His cheek twisted up into a sarcastic grin.

Allie's hand shook.

"Cara?"

"My net worth is currently four-hundred and eighty-six thousand." She glanced at me with fear in her eyes.

I smiled down at her. "Multiply that by one hundred and you have mine. And the family fortune is likely another twenty thousand times that."

Her face went pale. "No wonder someone is trying to kill me."

Yes. "Which brings us back to the Conti agreement. Ringo?"

He scoffed. "Don Conti's holdings are currently valued at seven hundred million in soft assets, and another five hundred million in the American holdings. But his bank owes one point eight billion in fines for money laundering. They're broke." He grinned and leaned into his chair, one arm draped over the ornate chair back.

Ellie stared at him. "What are you worth?"

"Me? Nothing. All my shit is tied to his. All the businesses, everything. Now that he's married, I'm shit out of luck."

"You own the estate." I reminded him.

"And the bills for it." He shot back.

"We'll adjust the agreement."

Firenze and Loppa squirmed. I needed to address that as well. "It was a clean shot, no?"

Firenze's jaw shifted. "*One in a million.*"

I glanced at Loppa. "What is your *objective* assessment?"

His face searched mine. "*If I weren't your grandfather's nephew and know exactly when he joined the family, I'd say he was born as one of ours. Yet, he stabbed you.*"

Allie followed the dual conversation closely. Her mouth tightened, and she glanced at Ringo.

My friend shrugged. "Occupational hazard."

"What are you guys talking about behind our backs?" Ellie mimicked Ringo's casual posture, but was much more on edge than he was.

I explained, "Signorina Jacobs, we mean no disrespect. It is merely business."

"My sister was shot at because of that business, *dude*."

"Yes, and her husband was stabbed, by that traitor." Loppa glared at Ringo.

"You stabbed him?" The conversation played across her face. She looked at Ringo, then Allie in horror. "And you married him for that?"

"Not for that."

"But… get it annulled. Duh."

Discreetly, I tilted my head to watch Allie's expression.

"We can't," Allie said, her cheeks pinked slightly.

Ellie's mouth fell open. Her gaze shifted to me. "You… dog."

She rounded on her sister. "And you…"

"Careful," I warned as Ellie stepped closer.

My wife's sister stared at me. Her expression shifted from surprise to scheming. "Allie? Remember what I said on the phone?"

Allie searched her memories, "We said a few things."

"Yeah, but, here's the deal. I can accept that your… *ugh*… husband has mad perks, but he's still just…well…not as scary as you think." She studied me with her eyes narrowed. Then blurted out, "It's-a-me-Mario! *There*. I said it to his face. Boo-yah." Ellie dropped an invisible microphone, then spun on her heel and strutted from the room.

Ringo's shoulders shook.

Firenze pretended to wipe his nose and stared outside to keep from laughing but the wrinkles near the corners of his eyes betrayed his amusement.

Joppa looked confused. Firenze quietly explained the reference.

Deep inside, I smiled. I'd count ridicule as acceptance.

16

ALLIE

Loppa wouldn't leave Mario's side while he and Ringo discussed the best way to approach Don Conti. I worried about his wound, but was also frustrated because Ellie was right.

I had a soft spot for *anything* wounded.

It made me pause outside the bedroom she'd been assigned. Between the villa's two stories, there were five doubles and the bedroom suite on the top floor that Mario and I shared. My heart skipped a beat remembering how sweetly he'd made love to me in the soft morning light that lit up the view, but kept our little corner of the hillside in shadow.

I swallowed that down and braced myself to confront my sister. Sure, she'd left on a high note, teasing both me and Mario with her little act, but I knew her better. She was hurting.

I knocked lightly. "Hey, can we talk?" I spoke to the wood of the door.

A rustle, and then the notable click of her lock sounded in the quiet night. The door creaked as it opened.

Ellie was in a T-shirt and soft yoga pants I recognized. "You're wearing my clothes."

"Duh, you've got all my lingerie."

Oh, right. "I can give half of it back if you want?" She packed so much, I could go two weeks without ever thinking about wearing anything twice.

Her eyes squeezed into slits of mistrust. "Half? Ew. *You* wore my underwear?"

I swallowed. This wasn't going well. I'd come to offer an olive branch, check on her simmering anger, not provoke it further. "I'm sor—"

"*Bish*. High five." Ellie stuck her hand in the space between the door and the frame. Her grin was wide.

I tapped her palm with mine, still hesitant.

She swung the door open. "Spill. Was it the flowered baby doll, or the slinky purple number that did the trick?" She fanned her face dramatically.

"I'm not—"

"Oh, come on. Which magic piece of lace tugged that stick out of his ass?"

Despite myself, I laughed once. My face heated.

"Big sis? Your 'husband,' he's *hot*."

It was my turn to fan myself, but I resisted. "We need to talk."

Ellie shifted so I could drop my butt on the double next to the already mussed up one. She shut the door and re-locked it. Her eyes traced my outfit and the state of my weariness. "Are you getting enough sleep?"

I shot her a look.

Her mouth curled into a tight, knowing smile.

"I should ask you the same thing. *Ringo*?"

"Don't go there. It was stupid. A rebound affair."

That's what had me worried. "Did you love Johnny?"

Ellie ignored my question for a moment or two, opting to stare at one of the paintings on the wall. "At first, maybe. He was…dangerous." Her eye roll didn't match the words.

Somehow, I had the feeling that Ringo had her ex beat by at least light years, if not whole universes. I kept that thought quiet.

Ellie picked up a thread of my question and turned it on me. "And you? You love…him?"

At least she refrained from using her nickname for my husband. I took a deep breath. "I've been thinking about that."

"You don't think about love, you just…love."

Her outburst was illogical.

"*I* think about it."

"You would," she shot back. And that was our biggest difference. I thought about things like love, what it was, how it happens, and she just…fell.

Yet, I'd fallen. I hadn't really been questioning what was budding with Mario. I'd wanted it. Badly. So much so, that I ignored many things.

"I guess I must love him."

Ellie flopped onto her bed and propped her chin on her hands to study me. "Why *must* you?"

"I don't know."

Her face twisted up. "You do. Think. That's what you do best, right?"

"But I can't think of why."

Ellie laughed, but her face fell into sadness. "Oh, Allie. Welcome to the dark side. Love just *is*. You can't think about it because it isn't something that happens in your brain. It happens much… lower."

"Don't be crude."

She rolled to her back and studied the ceiling. Her silent laughter stilled, and she sighed. "Okay, you love him. What's next?"

I mimicked her position, staring at the wooden beams that crossed the ceiling at irregular intervals. The house must be really old because the beams weren't perfect. And, the house was solid. The outside was a jumble of different-sized stones, while the inside had the cool coziness of a cave. Each window well was at least two feet deep. It resembled a squared-off castle running the length of the wide hillside terraces.

The distracting thoughts helped me to answer her question. "I don't know what's next. I feel like I'm losing him."

Ellie turned toward me to pay attention. "How?"

I shivered. "They're trying to kill him."

"Newsflash. Whoever that is? They're trying to kill *you*, too, and I'm not having it. Wake up, big sis. You need to get gone from here. Hide out, change things up. You can't think this one away, you've gotta act."

The plaster between beams was uneven, patched many times over the centuries. "If I do that, I lose him for real."

"And you don't want to do that, do you? I hate to tell you this, but you got it bad."

"It?"

"Love."

She made it sound so awful. And it was. Heartbreakingly so. If I stayed, the train wreck that had begun when he took my ride share was finally grinding to a halt. Something, somewhere was going to roll over us, taking everyone in its path with it.

"You need to leave, Ellie. Forget the vacation plans, just…leave. Do you what you do best and float your way back up to safety somewhere."

"I'm not leaving you here with them."

I took a deep breath. "You have to. I'm in love."

"You're an idiot."

Only my twin could get away with calling me that.

I studied her. She didn't say it with her usual bluster. "You didn't really love Johnny, did you?"

She shook her head. "Like I said, maybe at first. Then I saw him with this…bitch."

"Excuse me?" She knew how much I hated anyone using that word outside of its intended veterinary use.

She fixed her gaze on me, dropping all her defenses. "Allie, the woman was one of *those*. You know?"

No, I didn't, and I wouldn't indulge Ellie's assumptions. "Impressions aside, what did she look like?"

"Tall, polished, gorgeous… evil. You know that queen in Snow White, the evil one?"

I nodded so she'd continue.

"Think that, but…Italian. Mario's skin tone, hair color, long ass nose, but not quite so outdoorsy. Quite *indoors*-y if you get my drift?"

Dianora's face flashed through my head. "Curly hair?"

"Disgustingly perfect curly hair. And so fucking pampered. You can tell she's never washed her own dishes."

I'd gotten that vibe from Dianora. If it were the same person…

"How do you figure she's Italian?" There were more things going through my head, but I picked that question to ask first.

"Because when I caught them together, she was whispering fucking sweet nothings into Johnny's ears and he answered her back in Italian."

I blinked. "Johnny Pornstach knows Italian?"

Ellie shrugged. "I thought it was sexy."

A quick smile broke across my face, remembering a few of Mario's unguarded moments. *Yes*, it was sexy.

"Now I hate to even hear it, because—"

I finished her sentence, falling back onto the intuition we had developed from being together since before we were born. "Because you don't know what they're saying, right?" Loppa's hand grabbing my phone flashed through my thoughts.

"Yup."

I rolled to my feet. "Come with me."

"Huh?"

I tugged her out of bed. "I want to go look at the pictures again."

"Oh, Allie, do *we* have to?"

Yes. There was one grainy photo that I needed a good long look at. And I needed Ellie there to confirm it was who I suspected it was. Whoever was in the car with Johnny was a witness, accomplice, or possibly even the shot-caller.

But everything had been cleared from the living room. There were male voices coming from one of the offices which I followed.

Ellie and I snuck up to the closed door and leaned in. Our eyes met across the frame. "That's Mario," I mouthed.

"And Ringo," she confirmed with a whisper.

My eyes narrowed at his name. I didn't trust that man at all. They both were talking in low tones. Whatever they were saying wasn't in Italian, at least not in the cadence I was used to hearing. It sounded more like Mario's grandfather's dialect.

Which made sense. They were alone, in that circle, I suppose. Even though Ringo definitely wasn't Italian. His accent was too American, but tonight it was different. If Ellie hadn't confirmed it was his voice, I would have had a hard time recognizing it.

"No!" Mario's sharp tone cut off whatever Ringo said.

And damn it, I was being discussed, because I certainly recognized the word, "bride" in that sentence. Mario had said it enough around me to sink in. I closed my eyes to concentrate on the flow of words rather than trying to translate. He was angry, but in that controlled way of his.

Ringo wasn't much better. His bitter comebacks were sharp, argumentative.

Ellie tapped my arm to get my attention. She mouthed

something at me that looked like, "What the fuck are they saying?"

I shrugged.

Then Ringo spoke.

"You're not taking his place. Damn the code. You've got it good. For once in your fucking life, take the loss. We'll get him back without sacrificing you to that witch."

What?

"Your way would have my cousins, my uncles, *and* my grandfather in peril. This is on *me*. Not them. Don Manca will understand. He's the one who taught us: protect the family, protect our secrets, eliminate complications. The solution is simple."

"You forgot a big part of that section. It goes, protect the *home. Your* home. *Your* wife. Damn it, Mario. You *always* do this."

There was thunderous silence. My heart filled with fear. I knew I shouldn't be standing here as witness, right out in the open, learning my husband's secrets. But I *needed* to know them.

"Is that why you betrayed me?" Mario asked.

Ellie's eyes went wide. I held up a finger, so she'd keep quiet. It was odd how I'd picked that stupid gesture up from Mario so quickly. But it worked to keep her from barging in or making a sudden noise.

"I haven't betrayed you. I was protecting the family."

"By stabbing me?"

"Yeah. I knew you'd run to ground. Which meant you'd have help from the family. Not hanging your ass out in the wind and doing it all by yourself. We're a team, remember? Friends to the fucking end?"

My heart hurt for Mario, and surprisingly, Ringo. They both sounded so…wounded.

Damn my soft heart.

I motioned to Ellie to follow me. I took her almost back to the hallway before turning around.

"I'm sure the photos are locked up. I think I heard Mario this way." I deliberately talked loud enough they'd hear us approach.

Ellie picked up on my plan quickly. She sing-songed her mocking cadence of my husband's name.

The door to the study opened, spilling light into the darkened outer room. Mario stood in the span, his body casting a long shadow that stretched to my toes.

"Cara, you should be sleeping."

"Who can sleep in this place? The testosterone is so thick I broke my last vibrator." Ellie grinned at Mario flashing her teeth at him in challenge.

Ringo blocked the light to Mario's right. "You lost your vibrator in Venice."

Ignoring Ringo's rumbled barb at my sister, I asked, "May we look at the photos again?"

As the men stepped aside, Ellie shot a quick, "Dickhead," at Ringo.

"If that's all you want me for, I'm happy to—"

"Cease!" Mario turned one of the soft chairs toward me indicating I should sit where he'd arranged.

He was the proud, controlling type. Arranging people

and events to his liking. I'd missed that somehow. Even Ringo listened to him and obeyed.

I should be careful around him. Yet, I couldn't resist reaching toward him. I laid my fingers on the bare skin of his wrist. He'd rolled up the sleeves of his dress shirt, as if he were keeping the cuffs out of the viscera and filth he'd have to dig through with his bare hands in order to…

Protect the family.

I understood his place now. And mine. "Husband." I pressed two fingers against his skin so he'd know I was being careful with him, but also touching him. Because I could.

His eyes softened. "Amore mio."

Then the veil of secrets dropped over his expression, blanking it and making it much colder. "We've looked at the photos."

"Were you looking for a woman?"

"What?" Ringo asked.

"A woman. In the accident footage from the traffic camera." I pointed to the folders on the desk.

"It was two men," Mario insisted.

Ellie picked up on my thoughts. "Prove it."

Mario dug out the single photo showing the passenger of the car Johnny was driving, and the enlarged version.

"Look."

I tilted the picture sideways. While I wasn't certain, there was something about the gloves that appeared disproportional to the rest of the figure. "Ellie?"

She snatched it out of my hands and barely looked at it. "It's her."

"Her, who?" Ringo leaned too close and Ellie avoided him by sliding to the far end of the couch.

"Johnny's girlfriend. Or, lover, or maybe just partner in crime. I saw her at the club he liked to take me to. I suspected there was something wrong, and followed him… I also saw her coming from his house. The next m-morning —" She swallowed and continued, "The witch wore *my* fucking hoodie. That hoodie. It's my favorite because it's warm. I stole it from a football player I dated last fall. I must have left it at Johnny's."

Ringo snatched the paper from her hands and glared at it.

"You dated a football player?"

Ellie stuck her tongue out at him instead of replying.

Mario had to motion twice to get him to hand it to him.

"What does this woman look like?" Mario asked quietly.

"Do you have a photo of Dianora?" I interjected, trying to speed this up. I was tired, and if we could prove that she'd been in Chicago when her brother was killed, then… I assumed that would help my husband.

But the expression on both his and Ringo's face wasn't happy.

Ringo tapped on his phone and held it in front of Ellie.

She sucked in a breath. "That's her. The wicked queen."

Mario's eyes drifted from staring at the wall to me, then to Ellie. "You met her in Chicago?"

"Practically tossed her ass into next Sunday at the club where she was smearing her tits all over my boyfriend." She frowned and muttered, "Ex-boyfriend."

Ringo smiled. But Mario didn't.

His eyes locked on me. "Allie?"

I didn't understand what he was asking of me, but whatever it was, he'd exposed a major vulnerability. His body language spoke volumes. I stood, approaching close and gently pulling his face to mine.

His lips brushed my wrist and lingered there. "Protect the home," he whispered against my skin. His eyes locked with mine.

"Tomorrow, Loppa and Firenze will take you to a boat. You will cross to Sardinia. Understand?"

I searched his eyes. "No. Why are you sending me away?"

"Don Manca was kidnapped as he was leaving my father's home this evening. He's being held for ransom."

"Damn. This is like a movie." While Ellie marveled at the situation, I worried about his grandfather's health. Yet there was more than Mario was telling me.

"How much?" I asked. I'd pay it with my share of the inheritance.

Mario's eyes were black in the low light. "Not money, me."

"No," I told him.

17

MARIO

Questa vita che volevo darti si è sgretolata tra le mie dita. —This life I wanted to give to you has crumbled between my fingers.

Ringo stepped forward. "That's exactly what I said." He continued before I could argue with him again. "We will not pay a ransom, no money, no you. We'll go in our way. Eliminate the source. This is bigger than your problems, Mario."

My words were cold. "And sacrifice the patriarch of the family? Never."

Even as I spoke them, I pulled Allie closer.

"Don Conti wants me. That's all. It is a small price."

Allie tugged free. "The *hell* it is!"

She didn't understand—

Ellie raised a hand and pointed at her sister. "I'm with

her. And fucking Ringo here, go in guns blazing. Where do I sign up?"

These women were infuriating. "They want me. If that is what stops a war, then—"

"Hell no. We wage war, our way." Ringo's voice was almost as cold as mine.

Allie spat at him, "Who wages war? Him? No. You? You tried to kill him. You have no say."

"He's still family," I said, but everyone ignored me.

"No, he is not." Ellie crossed her arms. "Even *I* know that."

I spoke quickly, telling her what I'd told Don Manca, Loppa, Firenze, everyone… "He saved my life twice and didn't kill me."

Ringo threw a pointed hand in the air. "You know, I hate being talked around like this so I'm going to have my say right now. Mario, you *cannot* do this alone. I'm going to the uncles. I know I'm not wanted there anymore. But I know they all want a piece of that bastard. Even if his villa is a fortress. They'll follow your dumb ass in and mess this up permanently whether you want it to happen or not. Use your brain. Make a plan.

"The walls of Don Conti's office are reinforced with iron. The door is nine inches thick. It's made from two slabs of cypress banded around a metal core. There's three layers of security before you even hit the castle. Best way to get in is—"

"We are not starting a war!" I yelled. It would ruin us all.

Ringo stepped back. His eyes flashed as he searched mine.

"*Protect my home.*" I lifted Allie's hand, the one with my mother's ring on it. Then, I indicated her twin, forcing him to face the damage he'd done.

His eyes held pain I'd not seen since he was a student abandoned to the world with no home to return to when classes completed for the year. I'd taken him with me to Sardinia that day. He'd been mine ever since. I'd given him my family, my home, my life. We taught him a code to embrace when the world was too cold.

He studied me with those pain-filled eyes.

"*Are you sure, brother?*"

Ringo could protect Allie and Ellie. He was the only person who I trusted completely to do whatever was necessary to ensure their safety.

"Sì."

"Mario," Allie's tone held a note of warning. Even without understanding us, she knew I'd released her. I could see it in her eyes.

"Questa vita che volevo darti si è sgretolata tra le mie dita." I touched her hair before tipping her face to mine. "I swore I'd protect you with my life. I also swore to protect my family with my life. It is… honorable to live this way. I'm sorry."

Her eyes remained dry, but the tears were plain to see because her shattered heart was right there. I hadn't been careful enough with her or her family.

"You say live, but I hear die."

I tipped my head. She understood what I hadn't said. "Everyone dies."

Her mouth tightened, and her jaw was tight. "I'm not ready for you to die yet."

As if she could stop fate. I smiled.

"My heart." I brushed her hair away so I could touch her soft cheeks.

"I'm not ready." She fisted her hands in my shirt and shook me. The glint of gold on her finger drew my attention. I kissed it, reminding myself that life wasn't complete without dying. No one knew how long of a gift we were given. I'd done my share of shortening that span for others. I'd guided men like Ringo into that circle.

My mother died because of men like me. "Let me show you another photo."

She released me reluctantly.

I found what I was looking for in the pile of information on the desk. There were four photos in total. Two were taken from a sniper's blind. One was snatched from barely six feet away. The final one was too dark to understand the full image, but Ringo told me what the camera couldn't reveal. "These were taken in Venice, two days ago."

I laid them carefully, leaving space between the edges so Allie could see every detail.

In the first, Ellie laughed at a ragged juggler who plied his comedy in the Piazza San Marco. Over her shoulder, a man in a dark costume and mask stared at her, not the fool. In the second wide shot, the man who'd taken a seat behind her followed her as she moved through the square.

The close shot was of Ellie and her stalker. Someone

snapped the photo for them. She stood too close. Trusted too much.

That man died in an alcove between buildings, a victim to Ringo's vigilance.

Ellie inhaled a shaky breath. "How did you get those?"

I tapped the two shots that were taken from far away. "A cousin took these from one of the rooftops." I slid the close-up and the alley scene to cover the others. "These were from a member of the Conti contingent's phone." I laughed bitterly. "They thought you were Allie and tried create proof that my wife was unfaithful. They failed, miserably."

Ellie's hand moved to her neck.

I glanced at Ringo.

He addressed Allie. "Ellie was lured into a dark space and almost strangled. All because they thought *she* was you. When their hitman didn't return, and they couldn't intercept you when you fled Milan, they took Don Manca."

Allie's hand shook as she turned the darkest photo to change the angle. "Who took this one?"

"I took it. I searched the man I killed and found his phone." Ringo paused. "And I brought your sister here, so she'd be safe."

Ellie bit her bottom lip. "It's true," she whispered. "I thought it was just one of those dangers you warned me about but…"

As Ellie trailed off, I filled in the gaps. "If what you and your sister told us is true, Dianora killed her brother. She tried to kill Ellie in Venice. Likely ordered her cousin to make an attempt in Milan. You were targeted today. My grandfather is perhaps too important to kill, but his power did not stop them from touching him. They will not stop unless I stop it. They want revenge for Adelmo, and for the dishonor to Dianora, but that's on *me*, not you, nor my grandfather."

Allie met my eyes. "I don't know you, do I?"

"You know who I am. You knew when you approached me on the plane. You knew I was dangerous. That I'm an animal. But I'm not without honor. You and your sister will be safe on Sardinia."

She took a breath that shook. "Without you."

"Yes."

Her fist hit the desk, scattering a few photos. The binder with her careful travel plans slid to the floor and spilled the contents like blood. Her eyes dared me to fight her. "No. I've saved money, we pay a ransom."

"There is no money that can fix this." It was a matter of honor, pride, their wounded plans, and of a bitter family broken by too many power-hungry rivals. "When I go to Don Conti in exchange for my grandfather, my family will send all of these photos to him, and tell him that his daughter was responsible. He will see he has been betrayed. And, Don Conti is not a forgiving man. I pity his daughter."

Her head moved in silent denial. Those tears from her heart breaking gathered at the corners, threatening to spill.

"It's late. Go to bed. Wait for me. I want one last night if he is…stubborn."

Her mouth opened to tell me no. Nothing came out.

"You bastard." Ellie grabbed her sister and pulled her out of the room.

I tipped my head to Ringo, indicating he should follow them. But he lingered instead.

"I told you to live a little, not stick your head in a noose."

My fist tightened. "Like you?" He'd seduced my wife's sister and discarded her on my doorstep with no more care than he treated his whores.

My quiet words made him flinch, but he rallied. "No. You're not me. You care. You were born to care. I'm just a discarded blow-by. A mistake to bury. Eventually, I'll do everyone I know a favor and die, but you…shouldn't." He frowned, showing more emotion than I'd seen from him recently. "Maybe I should've killed you when I had the chance."

The quiet click of the door was louder than if he'd slammed it.

I spoke into the empty night. "You'd like to try again, wouldn't you?"

Firenze moved from the shadowed alcove where there was a listening screen hidden. *"He's going to betray us all."*

"It is a possibility."

"We don't have enough soldiers to counter that."

His words were true. *"His orders are to get my wife and her sister to Sardinia. Be certain they are protected if he changes that plan."*

"Sì, Don Valentini."

I stared into the shadows, counting my assets, moving the pieces around. No matter how I configured the plans, the solution was obvious. A trade was best for everyone.

Before I met Allie, it had been even simpler. Buy out

Adelmo, or give my promise to Dianora, then watch for the knife she'd aimed at my throat, survive. I would have kept true to a truce that had lasted over eighty years. I was willing to die within the strict confines of a code older than the bones of this country.

Within only a week, I'd followed my heart, and everything I knew, or thought I knew about living proved wrong. The desire to grab Allie, her sister, drag Ringo with me into exile, and hide from the assassins the Conti family and my own would send after us was calling me to ruin.

We'd last a month at most.

Don Conti knew precisely how to corner me. He embraced death by taking my grandfather. Everyone who'd been in this room knew his remaining days were counted on two hands only. No iron walls or modern security would stop the family from sending someone in. But moving quickly was a mistake.

A knife to the heart was much more effective than a war. And Allie had just handed me the weapon. *I* wanted to be the one who'd stab it into Don Conti's chest. Before he died, I'd tell him exactly how his oldest betrayed them all. She might believe she was ruthless, but she knew nothing of the word.

To kill her brother? It was a crime beyond dignity. The most brutal betrayal. And one our family would avenge. When the dust settled and the accusations silenced, my family would survive like they had for thousands of years. There was a reason the right hand needed the left. They washed each other clean.

I sent the images to my eldest uncle. He would see to it

that the families knew. In my message, I added the name of Ellie's lawyer so the network I'd built abroad would corroborate everything. There were two more attachments. The first was an amendment to my will.

I held up the marriage certificate so I could see Allie's gentle handwriting clearly. "I have a wife."

One I needed desperately.

Ringo stood outside Ellie's room. "They're inside." He slipped away as I knocked lightly.

"Allie?"

"Go away."

Funny how I knew that was Ellie's voice. "Send my wife out, Ellie."

The door flew open, and Ellie stuck her face between the gap. "What if I don't?"

I stared over her head at my beautiful bride. Our eyes met. Hers were rimmed with red. "Please?" I begged her, not her dragon-like twin.

Allie approached Ellie from behind and set a quiet hand on her shoulder. "It's okay."

"No, it isn't. None of this is okay. You're all a bunch of f—"

Allie's hand covered her sister's mouth. She whispered in her ear, hoarsely, "He's my husband. Let it go."

The mutiny in Ellie's eyes was plain. "Never."

Allie hugged her from behind. "That's why I love you."

Ellie patted her sister's arms as she glared at me. "Fine. Tell that bastard, Ringo, if I smell his cologne in this hallway one more time tonight that Loppa gave me a knife and I'm not afraid to cut his nuts off."

A shadow moved at the end of the hall. "I'm certain he already knows."

Ellie shook her head but let Allie join me in the hall. She spoke directly at me. "Seven A.M., she's mine again. Got it?"

"Understood."

She shifted her gaze to Allie. "Don't think tonight."

Allie smiled at her sister with more sadness than anything else. "That only makes me want to think—"

Ellie shook her head but smiled back. "Nope. Not tonight. Mañana, hermana."

"Bananny, hermanny."

With that, they hugged quickly before Ellie shut and locked the door noisily.

"Bananny?" I asked.

"Twin talk." Allie's eyes met mine. "Get used to it."

If only I had the time, I would look forward to learning that language.

18

ALLIE

Mario didn't turn on the lights like normal people do when they enter a room.

I hadn't noticed it before, but tonight I did. He stepped through the doorway, holding me slightly behind his side and blocking the room as he swept over the shadows in search of…assassins…like him. Something I really should think about despite my sister's orders. Yet, in a way, she was right. Tonight might be the last night I had with my… husband. Even if he survived, would I want to be entangled with yet another criminal family? I'd worked so hard to get free of that stigma before, I was foolish to do this again.

My heart wasn't listening, though. It was cataloging every move Mario made. It yearned for his warmth, his touch, the scintillating cadence of his voice.

He stood by the patio, waiting for a signal or simply taking the moment to observe his world without fear.

The night was clear. Starlight streamed through the

double doors at the end of the suite. The view beyond the narrow terrace overlooked the Gulf of Tigullio and Portofino where the glittering Mediterranean stretched to the horizon.

It was everything my childhood fantasies imagined, and more. Mario's silhouette was an obsidian cutout rimmed in silvery light. I approached, leaving the lights off and savoring his darkness.

His head dipped and I could make out the soft smile on his face, filling in the shadows from memories.

His voice was barely a whisper. "You are beautiful always, but the stars make your eyes shine."

"I—thank you. To hear those words from someone as handsome as you are, it seems unreal."

I didn't want to lose him.

The thought shot through me like a blade, and it cut deeper. It hurt so badly, my breath caught and my knees threatened to buckle.

Was this what fear felt like?

Or was it hopeless love?

"Cara…" Instead of the husky tones he usually spoke that word with, there was a note of pain. I knew why because I felt the same way.

"Please don't leave me. Please?"

His head dipped silently, but he rallied, sending me an intense message with his eyes that I couldn't understand. "We won't fight about this."

"The hell we won't. Going to Don Conti is…" Foolish, suicidal, dumb as all heck.

"I must."

Damn that code of honor. "He'll kill you."

Mario smiled crookedly. "No, he pays others to do that."

I pushed against his chest, but he was immovable. "That's not funny."

Yet his smile got wider. "Ironic, no? The assassin is the target."

My breath caught. "Why are you telling me that?"

He took a deep breath. "You should know everything."

I blinked. Something inside denied what I was hearing. I didn't want to know. Just like I didn't want to know why the nosy neighbors followed my mom to the grocery store, or to church, or every damn time we were dropped off at school instead of catching the bus. "What if I don't want to know?" What if I can't bear the burden one more time?

Mario shook his head. "It is too late for that. You are mine. And should I die tomorrow, what's mine is yours."

Oh fuck. "No one's dying, because you're not going." I took two steps back.

He laughed silently. "I am." His slow approach was meant to pacify me. I knew body language well enough to realize he was trying to soothe me like one would a frightened animal.

"Why? Why can't someone else go? Why can't your family get Don Manca out of there? I mean, don't you have competent people who can, I don't know, kidnap him from there?"

Mario's shoulders shook. "One of those competent kidnappers is me."

"*Oh—kay*, who else can help you do that?" My brain struggled to keep up with the revelations.

"No one. I will not have someone else's corpse sleep in my coffin."

That image was too vivid. My hands shook. I clenched them against my waist so he wouldn't see how badly his words terrified me.

"Allie, we have this night. It is beautiful, and ours. Please?" He held out his hand and took another step closer.

"Mario." My voice wobbled as his heat touched my skin.

His breath brushed my face as he slipped beneath my defenses. "I'm here. I want to love you."

My eyes shot to his face. "I'm already there."

His mouth fell open to a confused frown, then transformed to an enlightened oval. A string of rapid-fire Italian too fast to decipher spilled from his lips like a prayer. He saw my confusion and switched, saying, "My love. My life. You surprise me and humble me." His lips brushed my skin as he pulled me close.

I trembled in his embrace, not daring to unclench my arms but desperately wanting to seize his body and drag him somewhere safe I could insure he'd never be able to escape from me.

He noticed my fear. "My love?"

"How did this happen? I did everything right. I stayed out of trouble, I got good grades, I earned a doctorate, and I'm still—"

"Do you regret meeting me?"

I gave it enough thought to answer honestly. "No. I don't. I don't think I'll ever regret it. But I don't know how I'm going to live without you."

He sat down on the closest chair. His brow twisted up.

Pain laced his frown. His breathing was shallow. "I didn't think anyone would miss me."

I sat on his lap. "I will. So, make a different plan. Please?"

His eyes searched mine. "It would start a war. Many would die then."

Oh. I didn't want that. Don Manca, Loppa, Firenze, and even Ringo had grown on me. I couldn't and wouldn't sacrifice any of them… Well, maybe Ringo. The bastard hurt my sister. But the others? No.

They were dangerous, much more so than my grandfather, yet they reminded me of him. He loved us with his whole heart—Mom, Ellie, me, even Dad. Doted on us no matter the circumstances or stressors of his life. There were many families like Mario's and mine. Not exactly wholesome, but whole. Their love didn't stop at legal lines. It seeped everywhere. Even when it wasn't convenient, or wise.

I kissed him.

He was right. We had a beautiful night together, and I was wasting it by arguing with him. Or worse, trying to change him. He had honor, a code binding him to a strict course, and he loved his grandfather. Even more, he loved the family who'd pay the price if he didn't do what he had to. I understood that duty. Foolishly, I'd thought I could protect my parents and my sister by proving to everyone we were just a normal family. But the cracks were made before I was born. I'd only patched them enough to ignore them.

I broke contact before he could deepen the kiss and drug me senseless with his lips. "How about a plan that doesn't start a war, and you have a chance to come back to me?"

His smile was hesitant at first but grew. "I will do that."

Not try. Will. My heart sang.

"Come," I tugged him out of the chair and toward the bed. We had mere hours left. "I stole one of Ellie's nightgowns."

"You steal many more and she'll have none."

I paused at the edge of the bed. "I bet Ringo would like that."

Mario made a sound of disgust. "Let's not mention him tonight, please?"

Yes. I had better things to do with my lips and mouth than speak his name.

We connected again as I slipped free from my robe. His fingers traced the slim satin cords holding the shimmery fabric in place. The fabric was a soft blue, but shone silver in the night. It was so simple that it clung to my skin but flowed like water to my thighs where it ended without lace or other fanfare like her more daring outfits. This piece was something I'd wear if I had someone I loved.

And behold. I did.

Mario traced the satin with his finger tip. He paused briefly where the tip of my breast crested and the fabric fell loosely for a span. His body warmth contrasted with the chill of the night making the point he lingered over firmer and swollen with an ache that longed to be engulfed with his touch, or his lips. The high moan trapped in my chest pushed up my throat and lodged there as he slid his fingers lower.

At my waist, his hand flattened out and his palm caught

my hip to draw me closer. His lips met mine, and I forgot about everything except his mouth and the smell of his skin.

Then he slid his hand under the hem of the lingerie. It started innocently at my thigh where the fabric ended. But his fingertips curled inward, as if to grasp me like I was his personal Proserpina. Unlike that poor woman, I was fully willing. My foot lifted from the floor as I wrapped my leg around his, curving my body against him. His kiss deepened as his fingers crept higher, creasing the satin as he found only skin underneath.

He dipped his fingers between my legs. "*My heart?* Where are your underwear?"

I tried to catch my chuckle, but was unsuccessful. "I told you. I stole a nightgown, not her underwear."

"Madonna mia." His kisses turned frantic. My feet left the floor, and my back hit the bed. Mario hovered over me his lips spilling words too quickly to translate, but they were good words.

Between beatitudes, he kissed my neck. The nightgown was little more than a scarf caught under my arms as his hands roamed my body. His passion turned southward as his mouth covered my breasts with intense, open-mouthed kisses that devoured my senses and left me breathless.

He spread my legs wide, laying an evident trail of devotion toward his goal. His tongue honed in on my clit, and I arched off the bed as the zing caught me by surprise.

Of course, that simply helped tune his radar, and soon I was helpless and gasping, balancing on the edge of too much and oh-my-goodness not nearly enough. My fingers dug into his hair, not directing as much as clinging on for dear life.

"Mario, please?"

He ignored my pleas. My body quivered as my orgasm swelled. All self-control fled, and I screamed aloud as the pleasure hit an intensity I hadn't known possible.

I needed him. Now. I kissed him open-mouthed as I wrapped my legs around his body, giving him no opportunity to escape.

"My love?"

"I need you." Those words were foreign to me, yet they felt right.

"One moment, I—"

"Now, husband."

His eyes locked on mine. Something greater than lust lingered behind the questions there. He notched himself at my opening and waited there for my cue.

I pulled him close. "I need you. Just you." Nothing between us, no guard rails, no holding back. If this was all I had of him I'd take it with me with absolutely no regrets.

"*My heart…*" He sighed as his body sunk into mine.

My words echoed his. I spoke them in both our native languages, testing them, tasting them, and most importantly, owning them in every iteration possible.

Our bodies remained entwined throughout the night. It was as if my heart knew it was nearly time to say goodbye and wasn't ready to let go.

Even in the morning when Mario's soft kisses woke me, I clung to him, trying to drag him back to bed and remove the carefully pressed suit from his shoulders. He resisted me.

Brutally, I laid out my clothes for traveling and brushed my hair into a simple ponytail so it would stay out of my eyes.

Mario studied my movements. "Don't be angry with me."

I frowned into the mirror. "Then don't lea—"

"Don Valentini, it is time." Loppa's muffled words killed my hopes.

Please stay. I wanted to scream it so loudly it would echo through the house.

Mario kissed me one last time. It was only a quick brush of lips against my brow. "Loppa is coming with me. He will remain at the gate for Don Manca. Firenze is arranging the boat. It will take you and your sister. Do not remain here."

"You're coming back." I didn't ask. I demanded it.

Mario searched my face. A shaky breath escaped as he tried to form a reply. But instead, he offered more directions. "You will stay on Sardinia with Don Manca's brother. He has a villa in the mountains. It is guarded and safe. There is a doctor who visits. You will—"

"You are coming back." I willed it into being. I would not be alone. "*Then*, we'll talk about the rest, understand?"

"My love. If—"

No. I would not let him weasel out of this. He might have doubts, but I didn't. Not about this. If there was one man in this world who could arrange a miracle and avoid death, it was Mario. He was formed from men like Don Manca and that bastard, Niccolò Valentini. He had friends like Loppa, Firenze, and Ringo. I would accept nothing less from them. "We'll talk about last night and everything else when you get back."

He nodded, accepting my words.

But I don't think he believed in them.

Too soon, he and Loppa slipped away. The house held its breath waiting for violence that hovered at the edges of everyone's minds.

And I did what came naturally. I planned, plotted, arranged all the moving parts so that when it came time to move, I'd be ready.

But to move those plans into reality, I needed Ellie.

19

MARIO

Don Conti's home towered over the countryside and the Tyrrhenian Sea. The land was divided into minor villas and farm estates, with one exception, the ancient castle-like structure that once served as fortress, seat of power, smuggling hub, and most recently represented the crumbling grasp of a once proud family.

Four armed guards met our party at the gate. Their automatic weapons were displayed openly. Somewhere behind the thick stone walls guarded by multiple watch towers, my grandfather waited.

I walked in alone and stripped of any weapon they found. But my hands were intact. My tongue rested behind my teeth, and my calculating mind worked overtime to measure the distances, find the weaknesses behind the walls, plot rally points, scan for rust on the iron bars across the windows, and determine the fastest escape route out of this maze of buildings that clawed deeply into the hillside.

Over the centuries, additions had been added for comfort, or fashion. Only the main building and its attached kitchens and sub-kitchens and wine cellars were built for a full-fledged assault.

This fit my plan perfectly.

Don Conti's study sat near the base of the eastern tower. The staircase attached to the main hall but was narrow and twisted upon itself like a squared cobra. The hallway at the second-floor landing flanked a small balcony where you could see the room below or the rafters above. It would be an excellent place to position a sniper.

I logged that information as I entered Don Conti's office.

My grandfather idled on the couch. Near him were two guards, armed with handguns and knives, and perhaps more. His captors had taken his coat, his shoes, and likely stripped him before allowing him to wear the rumpled clothes on his back.

He appeared uninjured. That was good.

His face was carefully composed. The lids of his eyes hung at half-mast dulling the light lurking under them. He was placid, and plotting.

"Nipito." His endearment for me wasn't spoken with the usual warmth. It was as cold as a knife in winter.

"Grandfather." My greeting wasn't warm, but it held a note of civility that his had lacked. "Were you too slow? Or did you mean for them to catch you?"

"Shut up, boy." He spat out the command bitterly.

I should obey. The code demanded I respect my elders.

And yet, the code was also designed to remind men like

me that respect is earned, fought for, and handed out with closed fists and open eyes.

Standing near the fireplace was a solicitor from Father's arsenal. The stack of papers on the table next to him stank of his touch. They were another betrayal carefully plotted by an elder who'd grown too accustomed to politics and who'd forgotten love until it was too late to salvage the loss.

The four guards who'd escorted me to this place split into two camps. One pair guarded the outside hallway from invasion, and the pair inside took each side of the door as my jailers.

Don Conti enthroned himself behind a large desk. Behind him, his daughter loomed like a vulture. The wall at their backs was constructed of stone so ancient it was likely ripped from the foundations of the world. There were no windows or escape routes in sight. Fighting my way out of this mess would not be easy. With one reinforced door, four guards, and a maze of castle hallways behind me, it appeared hopeless.

But fighting wasn't the only way out.

"I'm here, release my grandfather."

"After I kill you." Don Conti glared at me. Scattered across his desk were photos of his son's dead body.

"For what? Those images lie."

The contempt on his face was obvious. "You are a coward, a betrayer, a murderer, and a perfidious serpent."

I could own the murderer title. Being called a lying snake wasn't as comfortable, but it still fit the truth. Betrayer? Unlikely.

Coward? Never. "I walked into your doors on my own

power. I was not dragged here, nor do I avoid my fate." I was not that word.

He tipped his head, as if barely acknowledging the woman on his left hand. "My daughter's marriage to you was arranged. You ran to my son to beg him to change my mind. And when he said he could not, you killed him."

"Hardly. I went to Chicago to offer a different bargain. Your son was unwise to refuse it."

Don Conti slammed his hand to the surface of the desk and rose from his seat to send his death glare at me more directly. "You killed him!"

The nearest photo had fluttered toward me, twisting as if Don Conti's will had turned it so I could see it better.

"Guns are the tools of amateurs. Your son was shot. I would not stoop so low."

"You lie."

It was time to change tactics. "Your American holdings are floundering because of poor leadership. Your assets here are frozen or locked in trust. Your banks owe fines you cannot pay. Your family needs three hundred million to remain operational through the end of the year. I offered Adelmo that amount, and an additional investment of one hundred and sixty million backed by Edward in Las Vegas if he simply signed over his American holdings. He wanted to discuss it with you, as he should.

"The next morning, I read of his death in the papers. They conveniently avoided the term, murder. I suppose that was your influence?" In the subtext of my speech was a threat. Don Conti, or someone in the family paid the police and witnesses to claim it was an auto accident. The death of his heir was unfortunate, but murdering his heir proved there was a hole in his protection. It meant his influence was weaker than anyone had imagined. In all things, Don Conti abhorred appearing weak.

"And you fled Chicago like the coward you are," he growled.

"I met with Edward to arrange a meeting with you. He has not reached out?"

"You murdered my son, you fled the field, and you spurned my daughter."

At the mention of her, I glanced up to read her expression. Her face was colder than her father's. An icy mask rather than rage. She watched me with unwavering intensity.

"I didn't know you cared for me in that way." There was no kindness in my tone. She deserved none.

"Enough." My grandfather rose to his feet. His guards tensed, their hands going to the weapons under their jackets. By doing so, they betrayed their dominant hands. I logged this information. "My grandson is married to another. We will leave now."

"The woman he married was involved in the plot to murder my brother," Dianora declared.

Don Conti pulled out another photo and laid it on top of the others.

In it, Ellie waited on tables. Her apron and tray provided all the visual confirmation I needed to know who it was without looking at the image more closely. Even so, my eyes scanned the flow of her hair from right to left. The softer arch of her brow and the curve of her nose confirmed her identity.

Another photo dropped beside it. Allie. She was on my arm in a sage green dress that flowed over her body like water. The gold ring on her finger prettily displayed for the world to see.

A final photo, this one blurry and taken from a great distance. The woman in it rode in a motorized gondola. On her right, Ringo sat in profile. His gaze monitored the surroundings for threats.

"This woman embedded herself at your side quickly, but spends time meeting with assassins who gladly accepted the job to kill you. Is she a snake you held to your bosom, or your accomplice?"

Don Conti barely paused before pointing at my grandfather. "Or is this part of *his* plot to destroy my legacy?"

The shift of Dianora's gaze to her father's outburst betrayed the hint of a smile tightening the corners of her eyes. She quickly remarked and pointed at me, but spoke to Don Manca. "Disavow this one and my father agrees to let you live in peace until your death."

"Daughter, do not speak for me."

Her face tightened.

Don Conti addressed my grandfather. "If, and only if, after your grandson marries my daughter and leaves me with an heir, a male heir, then he can live, and we will call the truce you suggested."

"I'd rather fuck death," I said.

In his anger, Don Conti swept all the papers on his desk to the floor. "That will be arranged soon enough!"

"I am married," I reminded the room.

"The papers." Don Conti addressed my father's solicitor who complied quickly.

"And, bring the woman in."

And with barely a breath, my careful plans unraveled.

Dianora smirked at me. "We caught your bride trying to escape."

My heart clenched.

Allie walked placidly beside Dianora's cousin, Leandro. Not that he gave her much of an option. His fingers dug into her arm. Her linen jacket was wrinkled, the blouse underneath pulled loose on one side. Her pants were stained with water and mud. There was a tear at one knee, and a darker stain from blood tinted the ragged edges. The neat ponytail she'd fixed this morning fell half-undone. Her head hung low, as if she were ashamed. She should not be. If anything, my guards should bear eternal shame for failing to protect her.

My hands shook with anger. I'd kill them all once I left this place. *If* I left this place.

She raised her chin and looked at me with tears collected at the outer edges of her eyes. "I'm sorry."

My heart ran cold. "You betrayed me."

"I didn't, I swear."

I bent over, carefully pulling the gondola photo from the disarray. "Tell me this isn't you with the man who is trying to kill me."

She barely glanced at the photo. Her mouth pursed into

a tightly locked chest of lies. It quivered with fear. She searched my eyes frantically.

"Tell me!" I shoved it at her, crumpling the page.

"It is."

I whirled on my grandfather. "You knew about this? Is that why you let yourself get caught?"

He stared at me. His eyes fully open for the first time since I walked in. *"If I had proof she was unfaithful, I would have killed her myself."*

That was enough introspection. I was a man of action, not remorse. "My grandfather will leave now. I will negotiate the rest of this truce."

"Mario, please, I can explain—" A soft hand hit my sleeve, and I shoved her away.

"Be quiet, *wife*."

"Be sure you collect your ring," Don Manca pointed at the band on her finger. *"It sits wrong on her finger."*

It did.

"Don Conti?" Grandfather paused, flanked by the guards escorting him.

"What?" The disrespectful sharpness in Don Conti's tone grated on my spine.

"The truce will be for one year only. We will renegotiate once I see my great grandson."

Don Conti smiled. "I knew you'd see reason."

A frown graced Grandfather's face. "Reason? No. You forget I come from a very *large* family. Many brothers. Many sons. Many grandsons. I can afford to let this one breed as he likes. But the others? They are not as forgiving. You will renegotiate in one year with *my* heir. I have many to pick from. You have…" he trailed off and studied Dianora for a moment before finishing, "…none."

My grandfather's chin went up, and his affected stoop straightened. His hands swung loosely as if he were in his thirties, not nineties. His guards opened the door to escort him out.

A commotion outside halted his progress. Ringo swaggered down the hallway, as if the men guarding him were his buddies, not his sworn enemies. He barely tipped his head at Don Manca as he passed.

"Traitor," I heard my grandfather whisper.

"Finish the job." Ringo's utterance was a single line from the code.

The full stanza echoed in my mind.

It did so in my grandfather's voice.

Don Manca fired words at Ringo's back. *"Finish this opera before it finishes us all."*

Ringo stepped inside the study and swept his eyes around the room. They landed on the woman who'd betrayed me. "Hey, honey, I'm home." Then he addressed Don Conti and tipped his head toward me. "Can I kill him yet? I want my payday."

"You followed him here?" Don Conti asked.

"Damn straight." He muttered the next part at me, "You're making this too easy. Again."

I ignored him. "I should introduce you to my wife, but I believe you already know her."

Ringo's crooked leer was wider than usual. His eyes traveled over the torn knees, the wrinkled suit, her disheveled hair, and with a lingering dip that fixated on her breasts, he answered me.

"Biblically."

Even the strongest of friendships could be tested beyond their limits. *"Do not speak about her in that way."*

"Sure thing, whatever you say. You're a dead man, you know that?"

"Not nearly as dead as you will be."

Don Conti clapped once. "Enough. It is crowded in here. You two, see that Don Manca makes it to the gates without delay, and Leandro, find out where this one slipped in through. Immediately."

With that command, he'd reduced the number of threats to my two guards, my father's solicitor, Dianora, Ringo, and Don Conti. My odds improved greatly.

Except for the imposter posing as my wife.

"We're getting an annulment, Ellie."

"It's Allie."

Liar.

20

ALLIE

Sea water and thousands of years of erosion etched out an arched cave under the rocky shore. The mouth was so low we scraped the top edge of the windshield as Ringo piloted the speedboat he'd stolen under the lip. Luckily, the grotto opened up to give the boat room to maneuver.

Ringo ran it aground on the yellow sand lining the bottom. The silt created a soggy beach that sucked in my boots within seconds of jumping free of the boat. Ringo ignored my complaints and told me quite plainly, "Quit bitching."

To which I answered with a good old-fashioned, silent finger-bird.

"I'm going to get your husband. Stay put."

"Take me with you." He'd threatened to tie my hands if I followed him, and I was reduced to begging.

"No, he'll kill me if I put you in danger. It's bad enough

I caught you outside the house in the first place. What were you two idiots thinking?"

Maybe divide and conquer, with a bit of switcheroo sprinkled on top?

"Besides, if I showed you the secret back door, I'd have to kill you. Or someone would, because I'm sure Don Conti doesn't want that information out. Now, let's repeat this again, what are you going to do while I rescue Mario?"

I tried one more time to get him to see reason. "Go with you in case someone's injured."

"No. Jesus. What part of Mario will kill me did you miss?"

"You tried to kill him. It's only fair he has a shot."

"I did *not* try to kill him. If I had, he'd be dead."

"You're so full of yourself."

"For good reason. Which is why you need to stay *right here* and let the *professional* handle it. An amateur might get your husband killed. Is that what you want?"

Jerk. Why did he have to rub that in my face?

"Fine. Go."

"And you're going to do *what* while I'm gone?"

"Stay here with the boat." I eyed it as it wobbled on its quicksand-esque perch.

"I have the keys, you know."

There went that plan.

"A little tip, I know people think I'm just another pretty face, but you shouldn't underestimate me."

"You're not pretty."

Ringo laughed as he slipped into an ominous dark crack near the back. His parting words echoed in the space long after he'd disappeared. "Good thing I can tell you two apart because you sounded just like your sister."

The rising water lifted the boat from its mooring and caused it to drift from the tiny beach. The light streaming from the entrance grew faint.

I perched on top of a dry pile of rocks, worrying about the tide. Was the water level going to get much higher? This was far beyond my comfort zone. And being left all alone without someone to rely on played tricks on my mind. I jumped at yet another strange noise.

Was that rocks falling?

It couldn't be. It wasn't nearly loud enough. But the slight clatter of noise that barely surpassed the roar of the surf outside had me searching the shadows at the end of the cave. I made myself smaller, wishing for the millionth time that Ringo hadn't abandoned me here. But if he hadn't, no one would be on their way to rescue my husband, would they?

The wait was maddening. No wonder my grandfather had married three times. No woman in their right mind wanted to stay married to a man who put themselves in such danger. And Jaja was only an accountant.

How could I do this? Moreover, *why* would I do this to myself?

Safe, sensible Allie Jacobs would never want a life like this. Last night's insanity slapped me in the face. I'd been stupid giving Mario my heart like that. It made me do dumb things like switch clothes with my sister, steal the keys for the sedan, and plot an escape plan…from mobsters no less?

And then what? Somehow sneak into a fortress I had no

clue how to find, in a foreign country, and free my husband without getting hurt?

Ringo was right. I was an amateur.

Another scrape of rock and a distinct crunch, crunch of footsteps, had me twisting around to discover the source. Sound echoed off the walls of the cave, making locating the source confusing. At first, it seemed to come from the mouth of the cave, but it also sounded near the rear of the cave. I stared at the darkness for longer than I should have.

"Mostri le mani."

Shit. I did a quick translation. Hands, demonstrate… damn it. *Show your hands.* A flashback of one horrible high school party and the stupid FBI agents who'd crashed it flitted through my mind.

I held my hands out and turned toward the mouth of the cave half expecting a police officer.

Instead, Dianora's cousin, Leandro, held an automatic rifle raised to fire. Adrenaline dumped into my system. I briefly considered racing to the back of the cave where Ringo disappeared, but knew that horse had left the barn even before my brain started on other options.

"*There are two of you?*" Leandro not only looked confused, but his voice betrayed his disbelief.

Two? I looked around. Then realized he must mean my sister.

"Yes. We're twins," I replied before my brain belatedly told me to shut the eff up. I winced.

His face scrunched, and his eyes darted as he translated my words. Then it cleared. "*That explains much.*"

I was getting better at this whole hearing the words and not translating them thing.

He stared at the back of the cave and the boat that floated out of reach. *"Are you…something something… alone?"* He didn't wait for my answer because he answered for himself. *"That bastard, Ringo."*

Oh yes, that was an expected response. I nodded along with his anger because I'd been thinking along those lines as well. That bastard, Ringo, left me alone here where Don Conti's men would find me. Or, that bastard, Ringo, grabbed the wrong twin and left her unprotected.

Wait. How did he know there were two of us? Unless…

Oh. That BASTARD, Ringo. "Where is my sister?"

Leandro's eyes narrowed. The barrel of the gun had gone slack but he aimed it at me again. "You will find her soon. Walk in front of me."

Oh… shit. Shit-shit-shit-shit…SHIT. Mario was going to be pissed.

I rose gingerly and struggled to ignore the stains on my pants as I stepped off my little mountain of rocks into the water-logged sand. Each footfall sunk about four inches and covered my shoes then made awfully rude noises as I tugged my feet out.

At the back of the cave, the rocks and sand were solid enough that it made walking easier. I couldn't pause to clean Ellie's shoes off because Leandro nudged me with the danger-end of his weapon. I couldn't see into the darkness.

"Move."

"But I can't see."

He muttered something derogatory about women, or

Americans, or American women. It was useless to try to translate because the tone he used said more than any words could.

But he lowered his gun, opting to brace it one-handed as it hung from its harness strap and he raised a flashlight at eye level with his freed hand. The light illuminated an ominously low and narrow opening. My shadow blocked some of the ground ahead, so I shifted to see more of the opening.

He grabbed my arm with his gun hand. His fingers pinched the muscles and ground them into my bone.

I dipped that shoulder to try to twist free, but that only made him dig in harder.

"Do not try escaping."

"Where am I going to run to? I can't see more than ten feet in front of me."

He stared at me blankly.

"Me, run? No. Can't see." I waved my hand in front of my face, indicating my eyes.

He shined the light right into them.

Bastardo. Now I really couldn't see.

A few other choice words ran through my head as I blinked my way forward and stumbled twice.

If he hadn't had a grip on me, I would have went down.

But we moved too slowly for his taste.

"You will not run."

He let go of my arm and went back to cradling the gun one-handed.

I rubbed the bruises he left and nodded.

Leandro shifted the light toward the cave floor. It had

sloped upward, but near the end of the space, another narrow opening was visible in his flashlight's beam. Once there, the path led to a staircase that must be ancient. The rock treads were worn into treacherously furrowed ruts sloping downward. I worried I'd slip each time I placed my foot.

Then it got worse.

The climb ended abruptly with a small opening I practically had to crawl through, and the cave opened up to my right. I went to my knees to catch my balance at the sudden sensation of space and the threat of falling onto stalagmites likely over hundreds of millennia old. Overhead, the ceiling was very low. The path twisted along the edge, carved into the wall, and around the stalactites that flowed from ceiling to their counterparts rising from the cave floor.

Leandro quickly caught up to me and put his hand on my shoulder.

I don't know what he intended, but I suddenly had a mortal fear of being garroted from behind, like Loppa and Firenze had illustrated so vividly. I spun, leaning into the pivot, just like they'd taught me. I came at him, swinging my fists into his crotch and working myself up to punching him in the face.

He doubled over, guarding his groin. His flashlight fell and rolled off the edge of the path, plunging everything into shadows.

I kicked out, holding onto the stalactite column next to me for balance.

Leandro wobbled, one foot slipping on the edge of the

path. His silhouette was outlined by the faint illumination of the flashlight that had fallen somewhere below.

I kicked again. He caught my leg, but the momentum I'd used tipped him over the edge.

My hands slid down the damp column, wedging at the base where I'd wrapped both arms around the narrowest width. My skin stung and my shoulders ached.

Leandro had a death grip on my leg.

My body hung over the edge and my breathing was tight because I fell hard on my side.

He called me a female dog in Italian.

"You obviously *don't… know… I… like… dogs!*" I kicked around with my free foot and found his skull with the last five words. I was thankful I wore Ellie's heavy boots.

My grip was loosening, and I kicked harder, cussing each time, knowing that either I'd get free or be dragged down with Leandro.

One of Leandro's hands slipped from my ankle.

I wiggled my whole torso to shake him loose.

"I will kill you, you American whore!"

I slid my free foot right down my leg to strafe his clinging hand with the tread of Ellie's boot. A horse did that to me once. I was bruised for weeks.

Surprisingly, Leandro had the same reaction I did.

With a cry and a loud noise, his hand slipped free and the strain on my arms lessened so quickly I thought I'd lose my grip just because I felt lighter than a feather without his weight. But I clung more fiercely to the rock column and waited almost a minute to risk looking down.

Leandro's flashlight was a small puddle of light at the

bottom. It landed in a pool of water, and the diffused beam made the stalagmites encircling it like sentinels glow like iridescent moonstones. In any other situation, it might be beautiful.

But I couldn't see Leandro. And not seeing his mangled body wasn't a good thing.

If he'd somehow survived the fall, he might find his gun and shoot me as I dangled over the drop. I had to get back onto the ledge.

The wall was uneven, giving me some footholds, but it was also slippery. With extreme care, I planned my next moves while factoring in how to maintain a tight grip on the column as I worked my body higher.

I tested each footing before I shifted my embrace on my rocky lifeline.

Eventually, I was able to wrap a knee over the edge to take the majority of my body weight, and I clung there for much longer this time as I rested my arms.

Then, with a final push, I shifted my hips over the ledge lip and rolled onto my back. I panted as I stared at the shadows that seemed to be growing overhead. The light from below was weakening. Probably due to water seeping into the battery casing. I needed to think about escape routes.

Once I left this room, I'd be blind. If I went higher along this path, I might find the castle, or slip over an edge like this one. One thing was certain, I didn't know anything about that route. And, I was weaponless and vulnerable. Should there be guards at the entrance, given the rare chance I even made it that far, I was sunk.

Yet, if I went down the way I'd came, I ran the risk of running into more armed men and be caught again.

Lastly, if I stayed here, and Leandro wasn't dead, he'd probably find a way to climb up like I did.

But I'd hear him doing that, wouldn't I?

The light gave out completely, and I was out of options.

Very slowly, I felt the path by my feet. Using my boots to feel around for the cave wall now to my right, and for the ledge to my left, I slid down the path on my butt only moving a few inches at a time.

When I ran out of path and only walls and empty drop were my options, I sat up and slowly traced the walls to feel for an opening.

But I couldn't find any.

Had I gotten turned around? Did I miss the opening?

Was I going to die here? That question scared me the worst. I hadn't done the things I wanted to do with my life because I'd been so busy chasing the things I was supposed to. Or thought I was supposed to do. I hadn't even been successful at that.

The darkness wasn't friendly. A light drip of water kept me company as I weighed the volume of my life and came up lacking.

Also lacking was any sign of life.

Surely, I'd hear labored breath, or groans of pain from Leandro?

The silence accused me and found me guilty.

21

MARIO

I scribbled my name on the dotted line and handed the pen to Ellie.

She glanced at Dianora before taking it. "Why are you doing this? I thought you loved…me."

"I thought my wife loved me, too. But apparently someone made plans without me."

"You can't hold that against me. I was coerced." She bent over the paper to sign her name.

"*Lying bitch.*" Dianora butted in.

Ellie snapped up straight. "What did you call me?"

"Sign the paper," I prodded Ellie, hoping to remove her from this insanity. Maybe if she wasn't a threat, then she'd be allowed to leave. And when that happened, I'd be able to do something horrifically dangerous. Hopefully, Ringo would protect Ellie over me.

I couldn't count on that.

Nor did I factor the unstable element that was Ellie Jacobs.

"I know some Italian words. Mostly the naughty ones. So…bitch, is it? Please. You were the one screwing my ex. You know, the guy who I planned to marry, Johnny Porciello?"

Ringo groaned. "Can we please do without the telenovela?"

Don Conti's eyes narrowed on Ellie.

"I got proof." Ellie reached into her jacket.

The guards snapped to attention, their guns trained on her as she froze in place.

"It's paper. Chill twelve-step and lunchbox."

As those who could speak English puzzled through the insults, Ellie slowly withdrew a stack of folded pages.

"See? Paper. Photos, mm-kay?" She plopped them down on the desk. The pages fanned open and everyone's eyes remained glued on the grainy image on the top. "There. One Johnny Pornstach with the fucking eco-boost Mustang I paid for wrecked to shit so he could shoot your homeboy."

Don Conti reached across the desk to unfold the pages. He stared at the photo for too long.

"This proves you were involved with my son's murder?"

"The fuck it does."

If I had any doubts at all of who wore my wife's clothing, I had none now. Allie rarely swore.

Don Conti glared at Ellie.

"Right. Look at the next one down. You might recognize someone in a hoodie." Her eyes shifted to Dianora.

"I should have killed you in Milan," Dianora whispered.

Ellie was genuinely confused. "In Milan?"

Dianora's eyes bugged out.

The solicitor, who until now had frozen like mouse trapped in a corner, spoke, "At the dinner. Right before Don Valentini changed his—"

I smiled. "Yes, I remember that. The money my father set aside for our marriage now goes to a trust."

"What?" Dianora stepped back, glancing between the solicitor and me.

"The four-hundred million he promised. It's in a trust you cannot touch."

Her mouth fell open

"You really shouldn't have sent your cousin after my bride."

Meanwhile, Don Conti compared the new photos against the other photos. Their addition filled out the sordid murder of his son. He pulled the image of Dianora from the pile. Familiarity, or simply the eye of a parent damned her. He placed the page flat on the desk and stared at his daughter. "Explain this."

"They are deceiving you."

Don Conti blinked once. "I know my own daughter." The room went quiet at his tone.

Despite knowing he wasn't as powerful as Don Manca, my blood chilled. There was death in the air.

Ringo felt it, too. He reached out. His fingers caught Ellie's sleeve and curled into the fabric, readying for action.

"Explain this!" He screamed so violently, spittle shot from his lips.

Dianora teetered on her heels, taking a step back. Her

protests poised to spew out as lies. But then, something in her expression changed. "You have two children, *had*." She corrected herself before plowing forward. "One who was *incapable*. Despite the best schools and the best closed-door sessions with you. He was a *goat*—no a lamb—readied for slaughter. He ruined us with his mistakes."

She shifted her argument. "And the other child? You ignored her, forced her onto your enemies with a command to marry and breed like a *cow*. I'm worth more than that. I can lead this family. I *will* lead this family."

"You will lead nothing. No one will respect you."

"They didn't respect Adelmo. But they'll respect me. They'll *fear* me. I'm your daughter. I'm just as ruthless, maybe more ruthless than you could ever be. At least I recognize weakness when I see it. Instead, you coddled it with my brother."

Ellie stepped closer to Ringo and whispered. "I can kind of see her point."

"Shh," he warned her not to draw attention.

Don Conti stared at Dianora as if he didn't recognize her. "I was wrong about you."

Dianora smiled.

Don Conti turned his back on his daughter to pick up the photo of her as she watched her brother bleed out. "You were a snake I should have killed when you were too small to bite."

"You bastard." Dianora reached inside her dress and pulled a pistol out of a hidden holster and aimed it at her father.

The guards shifted their attention to her a little too late.

Ringo and I struck as the shot rang out.

Don Conti stiffened. His body shuddered as if the echoes rippled through his flesh.

My guard hit the floor with his neck broken. I grabbed his gun and aimed it at Dianora.

Ringo's guard had his throat slit. Somehow, they'd missed his weapon. Ellie took one look at the blood pooling on the floor, and uttered two sounds, "Oh, fuh—" her knees buckled.

Don Conti staggered forward, one hand catching the desk to hold himself upright. He turned to face Dianora. "You are no child of mine."

Two things happened at once. Both Don Conti and Ellie fell to the floor. I grabbed the solicitor and pulled him out of the room as Ringo picked up Ellie and ran ahead.

Dianora saw us escaping and fired. I shoved the door partially closed and the shot bit into the ancient wood. The reinforced core trapped the bullet there, saving us all.

"Move!" I gave up on helping my father's man and ran after Ringo, who was hampered by Ellie's limp body.

He'd tossed her over one shoulder and had managed to steal the second guard's gun, but it was useless as we ran because his hands were full.

"Cover me." I slid ahead, hugging the wall of the curved staircase and leading the charge against Don Conti's security. The first guard I encountered had crested the first turn. I shot him in the chest, then jumped on top of his body, riding it down the final half-dozen steps as I fired at his back-up. With one more shot to the first unfortunate's head, I leapt free and fired two more shots into the mass of men who'd ran into the great hall.

Above me, Ringo laid down three well-aimed shots from the balcony, then hid his body from their return fire.

It gave me time to strip the guard of his gun and dive under the heavy oak dining table. I knocked one of the ornate seats over since the table itself was immovable.

It crashed to the floor loudly, and the men who hadn't been wounded split their attention to drilling holes through my shield and avoiding Ringo's aim from above. I crouched behind one of the two solid pedestals that held the table aloft and let them waste ammo for a few precious seconds.

Then I rolled from beneath the table, firing as I came up to one knee. The men dove for cover, and I slid behind the nearest body to secure his gun and felt along the line of his coat where I was certain I'd seen the hilt of a knife sticking out from under the flap.

Score. I pulled the blade and continued firing until the gun clicked once. Then I dropped that weapon and took the automatic lying at my feet. I laid down a line of fire that kept the men pinned until Ringo could carry Ellie down the stairs.

"Is she hurt?" My wife would kill me if something happened to her sister.

"Fainted dead away. She can't handle the sight of blood."

That was a problem. I quickly assessed the leaking bodies surrounding us. "We need to move."

"I got a plan." Ringo dipped his head toward one of the

picturesque windows. The tempered glass was so thick, it distorted the light streaming through it.

"Seriously?"

Our discussion was cut short by a brave guard who peeked his head around the column blocking my shots. I fired a short burst at him and sent him back into hiding.

"Then what?"

"Run?"

"Carrying fifty kilograms?" Ellie likely weighed slightly less than Allie, but they were matched in build and height. So much so, they could easily trade outfits and fool most of my guards.

"I've carried your dumb ass before."

I fired another round at the column. "No, you haven't."

"Slovenia ring a bell?"

A shot nicked the wall next to Ringo's head. He quickly fired at the figure in the sniper blind above us. Dianora ducked back into the shadows.

"Did you get her?" I asked to be certain of the urgency.

"Unfortunately, I missed."

I voiced my sentiment with a curse and muttered, "Plan B."

Ringo threw a leg over Ellie's body and fired at the corners of the large picture window closest to us. The glass spiderwebbed with his second shot, then he changed aim to the center, blowing a gaping hole in the window which caused the rest of the piece to crumble into tiny pellets.

The solicitor who'd followed us jumped through first, even before either Ringo or I could lay down cover fire. Dianora fired from the stairwell, and I pinned her in place with several short bursts before shifting back to the guards emboldened by her presence.

"Time to go."

Ringo threw down his gun and picked up Ellie, who was at the cusp of consciousness. Her eyelids fluttered, and her hands moved to grip his shirt as he tossed her around like a sack.

I laid down a wide swath of bullets to keep our hunters at bay. Once Ringo and Ellie were clear, I ran for the open window and dove through.

The landing was unexpected as the space beyond sloped sharply downward with grass so tall it hid the rocks and thorn bushes guarding the soft flank of Don Conti's estate.

But our firefight had one good outcome.

Loppa and the men I'd enlisted to protect Don Manca pressed from the gates and had secured the towers.

Once we climbed free of the brambles and met their party, Ringo handed off Ellie to the nearest soldier possible.

And as soon as his hands were free, I punched him.

"What the fuck was that for?"

"You dumb-ass. I gave you orders."

"I was saving you."

"Where is my wife?"

Ringo wiped the blood from his mouth. Behind us, Ellie muttered something under her breath that was aimed at Ringo. I didn't blame her at all. If the situation wasn't so dire, I'd kill him immediately.

"She's safe."

"Like this one was safe?"

Firenze approached. "Thank God. You found her. She ran from us."

If he said one more word, I'd hit him. "Firenze? I thought you were a smarter man."

He glanced at Ellie before attempting an answer.

"That is not my wife."

His surprise spoke volumes.

There wasn't enough time to set him straight. "Ringo? If Allie is not found in the next hour, you know what will happen to you?"

"Yeah, yeah… you'll try to kill me."

No. I would succeed.

22

ALLIE

Being trapped in the dark with only guilt and a dead body changes your perspective. After the initial panic, I panicked some more. Then I planned, second-guessed my plans, panicked again, and finally calmed down enough to think.

While I was thinking I had plenty of time to sift through my mistakes. Like thinking I could somehow lead a normal life. Or pretending that I gave two shits about what the local PTA thought about a mobster's granddaughter veterinarian. I'd been living lies.

No wonder my parents chucked it all and fled the city.

And no wonder Ellie developed a thick hide and a bitingly-sharp tongue to wage war against society.

Normal people never got trapped in a mobster's cave hiding from ghosts. At least not ones they'd created themselves. But that was the whole crux of this. I'd been fighting ghosts my entire life, but never truly living. I'd squirreled away the money I'd inherited instead of spending it.

Why? What was the point?

So I could be judged?

At some point, I began to talk to myself as I imagined going home.

I was deep in conversation with my mother when I heard the quiet squeak of bats.

"As if the darkness wasn't bad enough?" I asked the blackness.

My voice triggered a flurry of commotion as the tiny animals took flight and swooped past my face.

At first, I thought they'd traveled up the path toward wherever the path emptied near Don Conti's lair.

Then I realized they'd turned sharply once brushing past me and angled downward. Their distant whistles quieted, leaving the same emptiness of sound that had been slowly driving me crazy.

I held a hand up and felt along the wall, raising it as I dared to wobble to my feet. I hit my head on the ceiling as I did and quickly sat back down.

The ledge I was on crumbled slightly.

I scooted farther up the slope to find solid ground.

Once my legs could stretch out without hanging over the edge, I leaned against the wall to catch my breath.

"I came in through a small opening." It had been barely three feet high. I remembered stepping down as I crawled out of it, and also the way the wall tugged at my shirt as I squeezed through. Leandro had to force his body through because the opening wasn't wide enough for his bulk. That had given me time to turn uphill and wind around a pillar of rock and halt in place as the enormity of the chamber hit me.

I pictured the scene in my mind, thinking of how it looked and how wide the path was.

"I had to curve around the opening and turn left." And stepped down. Meaning that I'd passed the opening as I felt along the path in the dark because it was higher than I'd been touching.

Working slowly so I wouldn't miss it again, I swept my right hand across the path, testing the width before kneeling. The ceiling was too low yet. Leandro wouldn't have been able to squeeze through the opening if it was this short.

I moved about a foot before repeating my actions. Each time, I tested the height and then felt along the wall with my left hand as high as I dared to touch, feeling for a change in the wall.

Very quickly, I found the stairs. I slid down two before catching myself and sitting my ass down on the sloped edges.

"Ain't no way I'm walking down this."

So much for keeping Ellie's clothes decent. I was covered in mud and sand by the time the grotto opened up.

The boat still floated in the pool of water, but the tide had receded, leaving a long swath of disturbingly gray silt that spanned to the pool.

The FBI wasn't the only thing that had traumatized me as a child. "This is not the swamp of sadness."

I struggled to delude myself enough to wipe that image

from my brain. Yet with the first sucking step, I chickened out and decided not to try for the boat.

"Besides, Ringo has the keys. It would be useless and I'd be a sitting duck."

Remembering how quickly Leandro had snuck up on me, I worked along the edge of the grotto until I reached a point where the cave ceiling met the waterline and the sandy floor sloped too steeply to create a beach.

I braced myself for the bone-numbing chill of mid-February water, and was shocked to find it much milder than Lake Michigan's polar chill.

Before I could talk myself out of it, I swam through the opening and kicked toward the light.

The water was less choppy than it had been earlier, so I wasted no time paddling to the nearest point of the rocky shoreline.

Looming above me and slightly south was a squat tower. It reminded me of a casemate, armed to the teeth and ready to annihilate anyone storming the hill. I had no plans for that. Moving quickly, I found a secluded flat rock that tucked behind a stand of scrubby trees where the wind was non-existent and the tower was completely hidden. There, I stripped off the outer layer of wet clothing and wrung the excess water out. Ellie's boots were next. I pulled the wool socks off and stuffed them over a pair of branches so they'd dry quicker. They were technically mine. And as soon as they were remotely dry, I'd put them back on.

The sun was warm and the sky clear. If Ellie were here, she'd likely suggest sun-bathing. As crazy as it sounded, it wasn't a bad thought. Wet and cold would kill you faster than dry and cold. And for someone used to Chicago winters, this little sun beach was downright balmy.

Through all of this, I kept an eye on the shore and the ocean. I had a fairly good view of the southern curve, but the northern slope was too steep and blocked the shoreline.

I decided it was a good thing. Even here, the bluffs were sharp and the terracing that normally accompanied civilized coastline was abandoned. It was like perching on the edge of the world during some forgotten time.

With a castle tower, armed mobsters, and one very MIA assassin.

A voice drifted from the beach below. I barely heard it over the surf, but then an equally male voice answered it.

I knew those gravely tones and stretched my neck to spy Mario and Ringo moving over the rocks by the cave entrance.

"Why did you think she'd be safe here?" Mario pointed at the tower that had frightened me so. "They would see her."

"Relax. She's in the cave."

No, she wasn't. I almost gave myself away, but waited to see what Ringo would do next.

Instead of diving into the water, he crawled between some rocks and disappeared from sight. Mario reluctantly followed him.

I gathered my things and put on what I could without courting hypothermia, and scooted down the slope to where they'd disappeared.

Between the rocks was a narrow stairwell formed naturally by the jumbled stones, but obviously assisted by human means. The larger boulders formed walls and I followed the sound of their voices as I climbed down the uneven riser intervals.

"She was here; I swear it!"

I emerged from a final twist farther into the cave than I'd anticipated.

Mario held a gun on Ringo. "You…" he struggled for words. "I trusted you, I *begged* you to keep her safe. You swore to me on the code you would protect her." He spoke rapidly in Italian, or the Galluric dialect that his grandfather preferred.

"Mario, please…listen to me."

I cleared my throat before this got any worse. "Ahem, boys? Can we leave now? I'm cold."

Mario whipped around, gun still half-raised. But as soon as he saw me, he dropped it into the sand. "Cara mia."

I don't know if I ran to him, or he ran to me, but we closed the gap between us faster than I could blink. I wrapped around his warmth, soaking it in and likely chilling him but neither of us cared much for the logistics. Instead, he kissed me frantically and held me with a ferocity that would have frightened me if I weren't so damn grateful he was alive. I even mused aloud. "You're alive."

His lips stalled on mine. "I am, and you? Are you hurt?"

"I'm cold but whole."

"How did you get wet?" He tried to make some distance between our bodies to study me, but I wasn't having it. I wasn't ever going to let him go again, and more importantly, he was warm. And I'd finally begun to shiver from the chill.

"Long story short, I—" Did I dare tell him about

Leandro? He'd lose it and probably kill his best friend if I let that slip right away.

"I didn't know about this entrance, so I swam out."

"You could have died." Mario stripped off his suit jacket and wrapped it around me. I protested since I was wet, but it quickly got shot down as he hurried me out of the cave and into the sunlight.

Mario flagged down a party in the distance. Loppa and a couple of Don Manca's guards joined us as we climbed the hill toward a cluster of cars, a bunch of armed guards, and my sister who stood beside Don Manca.

"You were supposed to stay inside." Ringo muttered as we neared the cluster of men. Some of them were not Don Manca's men and I recognized at least one of the guards from that ill-fated dinner party in Milan. Eight of them were on their knees and being watched closely by Don Manca's men.

"It got complicated. I'll tell you once we're far away from this place." *And I'm warm.* Although my chattering teeth wanted to claim I'd never be warm again.

A thin, older man with glasses approached Mario. "A moment, please?"

Mario's frown should have scared him off, but I guess lawyers were immune. "Speak quickly."

"I wish to contact the authorities about Dianora's crimes and her father's shooting. With your permission of course. Don Manca believes it best we work with them to locate her and her cousin."

Dianora was missing? And her father was dead? What had Mario done?

"And the others?" Mario pointed at the estate.

"I will tell them it was Dianora. A rebellion. Strictly an internal affair I was unfortunate enough to witness. Don Conti is still alive, which adds weight to my words. He wants her found."

Mario searched the cars to make eye contact with his grandfather. Don Manca dipped his head once to convey his agreement.

"Make certain you remove any mention of my wife or her sister. Understood?"

"I understand completely, Don Valentini."

He shuffled away, directing the men left behind to help him with the arrangements.

Meanwhile, a procession of cars whisked us away. They wound through the countryside and farther inland to a medium-sized regional airport. We boarded a small plane that flew southward and then away from the coast.

It touched down at the Alghero–Fertilia airport in Sardinia. From there, the procession progressed until we were safely ensconced in Don Manca's territory.

The warm bath felt good, but the fireplace and a warm Ponce Livornese heated me both inside and out.

Ellie joined me. She had one of the tiny cups of espresso-tinged alcohol in her hands and inhaled the spiced aroma several times between sips.

"Is that your first or…?" I'd had two and was feeling the effects.

"Second. The first one went down too quick. I'm savoring this one."

I wish I'd done that. A third would knock me right out

despite the caffeine, and two didn't feel like enough. "What a day."

Ellie made a noise that sounded like agreement, but was closer to a grunt. "I don't want to think about it."

I leaned to prop my head on her shoulder. "I know."

She jostled me a little when she finished her sip. "At least you didn't faint."

"I'm sorry you got kidnapped."

She hummed briefly, considering her words. "I guess I'm sorry you went swimming. It was cold, wasn't it?"

I gave her question the thought it seemed to deserve. Maybe that was the rum? "Remember the lake we went to in Wisconsin that one summer? How cold it was?"

Ellie shivered. "Spring fed and eighty feet deep. Fuck that."

"Just a smidge colder."

Her shudder dislodged me, and I wrapped a quilt around us both. Then, pulled her close so our positions were reversed.

Someday, I'd tell her the whole truth. But not until I had a chance to apologize to Mario for being a judgmental idiot.

23

MARIO

If not for the sharp curl of Ellie's hair falling to the left, I might not have been able to tell which twin was my wife. The fire had settled into cozy embers and their bodies were wrapped tightly together so only the bridge of their noses were visible.

Ringo elbowed me. "Left." He mouthed. Meaning, I should take the woman on the left.

I pointed to Allie and smirked. "Are you sure?"

He lifted his middle finger at me, a gesture he'd never outgrown. Then he tugged the blanket free and pulled Ellie out of her sister's sleeping embrace.

Instead of doing the same, I settled next to my wife and covered us both with the quilt they'd been huddled under.

She was awake, but still in that soft, non-verbal state where it would be easier to let her drift back into sleep. But I was not one to travel a cowardly path. I wrapped my hand around hers and felt the fingers until I confirmed she was wearing my ring.

"I am so very sorry about today," I said.

Her head lolled to rest against my chest. I felt her eyes searching me for answers, so I elaborated.

"You were right. I shouldn't have left you. I should have let the others make better plans." I just couldn't, though.

"Did they find Dianora?"

I nodded. Once we reached Don Manca's, and I saw to Allie's comfort, we'd locked ourselves into a war council that kept close tabs on Don Conti's condition, and the tentative truce. Dianora was located about ten miles from the villa. "Her cousin is still missing, however." That concerned everyone.

But there was little we could do except guard the family, and insulate Allie and Ellie from the danger as much as possible. Perhaps Leandro was resourceful enough to make his way here, but he was not intelligent enough to slip through everyone's vigilance and strike us at our heart of power.

At least that was the consensus. But I still made plans in case he defied the odds.

"Ellie says she signed annulment papers."

I smiled. "She used her name." They would not be valid. Yet…

Would Allie leave me now? I bit down on my fear. "My father's solicitor has copies. Unsigned."

Allie stared at me. Her face was uncharacteristically somber. It went far beyond her usual seriousness. The softness that graced her eyes was missing. "I need to tell you something, and I need you to promise not to get angry."

"Cara, I…" I would not get angry. I'd be heartbroken. "Today, I realized that I couldn't live without you. I wouldn't want to. I knew it was my death by going to Don Conti's, but I thought it would keep you safe. And when I saw your sister, for a moment, I thought it was you and—"

Her fingers covered my mouth. "Mario? Shut up for a minute, okay?"

I nodded, helplessly.

"I love you."

Why did that sound like she was going to say goodbye?

"I love you—"

Her fingers tightened until her short fingernails tapped my lips. "If you keep doing that, I'm going to get pissed off. Shh…"

I swallowed the fear that had crawled up my throat.

"You are not going to get angry, right?"

I nodded.

So help me God, I would never be angry with her.

Allie took a deep breath. She let it out with a sharp, "Okay. When Ringo left me in that cave—"

I growled, remembering how cold she was when we found her.

She leaned back and squared off against me. "You promised not to get angry."

"I'm not angry with *you*."

"Okay, new promise, you will not get angry at Ringo, got it?"

I refused to answer.

She stared me down until I begrudgingly agreed. "I won't get angry-er."

Allie pursed her lips and worked through my reply. "Fine. I'll just rip this Band-Aid off. You can't find Leandro because he is at the bottom of some pit in that cave that leads up the slope to Don Conti's castle. Ringo snuck up there to save you, and Leandro found me. I kicked his ass."

For a moment I couldn't speak. Part of my gut fell into a dark place that was half horrified, and half stunned. The rest of it tried to rein in the emotion that goaded me to hunt Ringo down and gut him. "You kicked Leandro's ass?" It came out as a whisper because my throat was not working right.

"Yes. Well, technically his head… and face… and I think I kicked him in the nuts. No wait, I hit him there. Got him good, too."

If I hadn't been sitting, I would have fallen.

Allie continued, oblivious to my turmoil.

"Remember when you caught Loppa and Firenze teaching me how to defend myself?"

I nodded, absently. They attacked her from behind.

And with a snap of realization, I knew. The scene played vividly in my mind. Leandro was more than twice her weight. He'd had to have been lower than her for her to be effective.

"You struck him?" I picked up her hands and searched for bruising. The dirt she wore earlier masked it, and the scrapes that marred her skin. I tugged the cuffs of her loose sleeves up and marked the long string of bruising that spanned from the heels of her hands to well beyond her elbows.

"You're not getting angry, right?"

I breathed deeply. It leaked out slowly as I set aside murderous thoughts. "I'm not angry with you."

"You can't get angry at Ringo, remember?"

I did.

"Where is Leandro's body?" I asked.

Allie frowned. "Ringo says it's a secret entrance and that Don Conti would kill to keep it that way, so…should I tell you?"

I closed my eyes and opened them slowly so I could master the emotion that betrayed me. "I have no secrets from Ringo." And that was damning. He held secrets from all of us. He could have told me about the secret entrance the night we planned.

But I wouldn't listen to him. He hadn't been against attacking the castle, only against me going in alone or through the front door. He knew how thick the office doors were. He'd been there before. And I hadn't bothered to wonder how he knew.

"Should I tell you?" she asked.

I searched her face. The warmth in her eyes had crept back in, but it was wary. I didn't blame her. "If you want to keep that secret, I can't stop you." Nor could I stop her from leaving me. My life was too violent for her gentle nature.

"I'm not going to keep secrets from you. Not now, not ever. I don't want to live that way." She stared at my face. "I love you."

"Why?"

She searched her thoughts. "Well, you didn't bat an eye when I dropped a big bombshell like murder on you."

"Self-defense. You are incapable of murder."

"Wanna make a bet?"

I laughed silently. She'd lose. Perhaps she was capable of murder, but only for the best of reasons. Like protecting her sister, or protecting someone else she loved.

And like a whip that thought circled my mind and snapped back at me. "You love me?"

"Yes."

Another piece of the puzzle fell into place. She'd gone searching for me. Firenze explained the morning's events to me.

The twins swapped clothes shortly after I left with Loppa.

Allie, dressed as Ellie, slipped into the garage and tried to take a car. When confronted, she fled down the hill toward the town. Meanwhile, Ellie, dressed as my bride, ran across the slope toward the walking path she'd come up with Ringo. It was there she'd been taken by Dianora's crew before Firenze could catch up. He couldn't fire on the group because they used Ellie as a shield.

Ringo, perhaps recognizing the difference between the twins, followed Allie and fled with her by boat when the villa was compromised.

"I love you. I couldn't let you turn yourself over to that bitch. And it's not just because she's competition, it's because you'd be miserable. And I'd be miserable, and she'd win." Allie took my hand and squeezed my fingers.

"And that idea sucked. I want to be happy…with you. I want *you* to be happy. And if that's with me, well…"

I pulled her close. "I love you, my beautiful bride."

"Are you sure?"

"Certain. I love you more than flowers love the sun. More than the water loves the shore. More than any man has loved a woman before. You are strong, resourceful, kind, giving, beautiful, smart, and I'd be the worst fool in the world not to love you as faithfully and deeply as I could for as long as I possibly can. You are more than I ever dreamed of. I'm incomplete without you."

I searched her face for truth that my words moved her.

The corner of her mouth lifted. "You had me at flowers." She broke into a wide grin.

My heart soared. "You really love me?"

"I do. And if you're done putting yourself in danger, I'm on board."

A scoff broke free. "Please. Devlin's the one who loves danger. I love plans, rules…"

"Your code?" Her tone was careful.

"You. I love you." I leaned in to kiss her, but she avoided my lips.

"What about your family?"

"What about them?"

"I mean, your father isn't exactly my biggest fan. And your grandfather might be a little angry about being kidnapped."

Her worries were unfounded. Father risked his best lawyer. And Grandfather? He was luxuriating in the possibility of taking over all of Don Conti's holdings.

"Let me tell you about the code."

Allie settled closer and gave me her attention. In moments like this, I still marveled at how well she fit me. Her quiet intelligence and her peaceful strength were tuned to my temperament perfectly.

"When you fall in love, your bride becomes your number one priority. Over family, over everything else. We are a proud people. But we'd not have existed without love. The woman is the core of the family. We honor her." I paused, remembering how Grandfather pointed to his wife. She'd smiled to herself, a blush creeping up her cheeks.

"Family, women, honor, and wives appear often in the words I live by. But until I met you, I didn't understand how someone so gentle would fit."

"I'm not gentle."

This woman… she made me smile. "You are. And that's why I trust you with my life and my family, and most of all, with my heart."

Her eyes glistened with unshed tears. "You mean that, don't you?"

"I do."

Sempre. Forever.

24

ALLIE

"Are you sure you don't want to stay?"

Ellie bit her lip and stared at the blue waters of the northern Sardinian coastline. Even as early in spring as it was, the ocean was a postcard-worthy vista of pristine beach, turquoise-hued ocean, punctuated with dangerously rocky coves that were perfect recreational grounds for smugglers and snorkeling.

Don Manca's estate spanned almost as far as one could see between the two arms of headland that marked the boundaries of the family's holdings on the eastern and western edges. To the north was the Mediterranean ocean, a string of rocky islands, and eventually, Corsica. To the south there were farmlands, small villages, and a thousand families, or perhaps more, who all bowed their heads as Don Manca passed by. Their words of greeting to him were reverently soft with a hint of awe and maybe a little love. They gave Mario almost as much respect. Even the local law enforcement treated him with respect. It was a far cry from my childhood memories and the stalking I'd grown to fear.

Just a short boat ride away was a nature preserve with hiking and scenic views from the cliffs. Beyond that, there were a myriad of million-dollar estates owned and populated by the elite few who could afford a slice of this wild island. There were lavish resorts, spas, nightclubs, and all the glitterati Ellie could handle.

If she'd just get over herself.

"I can't stay," she said.

I knew why—that damn Ringo Devlin.

"You really should have a bodyguard." Just being my sister and looking like me made her a target, despite the fact that we'd come out on top of this mess and the threats to Mario eliminated.

"I don't *want* a bodyguard. I *want* to be as far away as possible from Italians and mobsters and all this crap."

Did I blame her? I'd been there myself.

But something shifted while I was trapped in that cave. I'd finally found my courage. Or maybe decided I didn't like living like I was dying all the time. I wanted to grab onto Mario and his family, and *my* family for all the good and the bad of it. Which was why I really didn't want Ellie to leave. But she was miserable here.

"Where will you go?" I asked quietly.

She shrugged. "I don't know. That's the best part. No one can track me if I don't know where I'm going, right?"

I nodded, hesitantly. Even now, I itched to map an itinerary for her.

"Don't be like that. I'm good at this. I'll be fine.

Dianora's locked up. There's no one running the Conti family who can pay anyone to hunt me down." Ellie hesitated. "But if there were, they would target Mario, we're not interesting enough for them anymore."

"Thanks for the backhanded compliment."

Ellie tugged my hand. She twisted it around until she made the ring catch the light just right. Her finger rubbed the crest engraved into the flat oval. "Power. That's what people want. Not me. I'm nobody."

That wasn't true, but I'd try to give her as much protection as I could without smothering her. "Mario and I will be in Rome for a week. Then we're going to Amalfi, and —" Our plans were to flaunt the wedding, put both of our faces into the spotlight with his father's network, and let the paparazzi or whoever was interested target us until the novelty wore off.

Ellie slapped a hand over my mouth. "I know your plans. He wines and dines you on the honeymoon you should have had. You're his show pony for four weeks. And you get your grand Italian museum vacation. I got it."

I brushed her hair back so I could wipe the moisture threatening to spill from her eyes. "Be careful."

Ellie snorted. "That's my line. You're going to need it around these bastards."

"Don't call Loppa that. He's a sweetheart."

His head dipped slightly, just enough to acknowledge he'd heard us.

Ellie stared into the shadows. "If only I'd met you first," she told Loppa.

"I would not leave my wife."

"My poor broken heart." She fake-sobbed.

I caught my giggle just in time. Ellie was too dramatic. The gold ring on his finger was practically embedded there with age. "Stop flirting."

"Never." Her smile faded too quickly.

"You could stay." I tried to keep the longing note out of my voice. And I didn't want it to sound like a question.

"I'd rather gouge my heart out with a spoon. No thanks."

Beyond Loppa was another shadow. Ringo lurked there. Far enough away that Ellie couldn't touch him, or take a swipe at him if she got too angry, and too close to let my sister breathe.

I hugged her.

"I'm only going to ask that you come back in time for the celebration. I need a maid of honor to put on display."

"You're going to make me wear pink, aren't you?"

I shook my head. She'd look washed out in pink.

"Little flowers on a creamy beach dress that is too virginal for words?"

Damn it. *Yes.* "Naw." I could picture her face once I sprung it on her, though.

Ellie tipped her head. "Any color, as long as it's black… or bright red. Understand?"

I waited for her to get nervous.

"You're not putting me in pastel."

Technically, it wasn't pastel. More… "airy" than that.

Her eyes rolled. "Allie…" It was as if she could read my mind.

Which meant I had to set her straight. "You dressed me in nude brothel wear."

"Hell yeah. I'll wear that."

I cleared my throat reminding her she had no choice. "It's *my* wedding party this time." Besides, Mario's bloodstain was set into the fabric by this point. She'd faint if she saw that.

"Right." She grinned with teeth showing to prove to me she was trying, but wasn't on board with my vision. After a moment, it fell. "Okay. I'll be there. Unless of course some hot foreigner kidnaps me and forces me to fly away with him on his private jet." Her hand flew to her forehead dramatically. "Death by sex, how traumatic."

A voice from the far shadows muttered, "That can be arranged."

"Shut the fuck up, Ringo! No one asked you."

I kissed her quickly, because I didn't want those two arguing again. "Firenze is waiting." I glanced at the dark SUV in the circle driveway. Her chauffeur-slash-bodyguard waited beside it.

Only two suitcases were in the trunk. She'd bequeathed the lingerie to me.

She hugged me tighter. "I love you, big sis. Be deliriously happy."

"I plan on it." I'd be happier if she were that way, too. But until she got over Ringo, that was not a possibility.

As soon as Ellie let go, Mario wrapped an arm over my shoulders. "I'll insist she is."

"Good luck to both of you. Enjoy *my* clothes." Ellie flounced away, giving Mario a sly wink.

Firenze frowned. He let her settle in the back seat and then walked over to stand in front of Mario. "To confirm, I have the right one, sì?"

I could feel my husband's silent laughter. He squeezed my shoulder. "You put your ring on wrong this morning, Allie."

I jabbed his rib cage in jest. "Ellie," I teased.

Poor Firenze looked worried.

Mario sent me a cautionary warning with his eyes. "Allie. I know my wife."

"You think so?"

His eyes raked down my body. "Every inch of her."

I brushed the hair away from Mario's brow. "I love you."

Our lips met softly.

Mario hesitated before deepening the kiss. He brought my hand up so Firenze could see the sigil that wasn't turned the wrong way. I shook his hand off and threaded my fingers through his hair, practically climbing into his body.

Firenze cleared his throat. "Thank you for confirming, Don Valentini."

"Idiot."

Mario broke the kiss to glare at Ringo.

His friend growled out a reply. "He should be able to tell them apart by now."

"They are identical twins," Firenze shot back.

"Not identical." Mario touched my eyebrow and the curve of my hairline. Then, the sharp tip of my nose. "Ellie has a rounder face, and her hair swings to the left not the right."

"That's how you know?" I asked.

"There are other ways to tell. But those are for *me* only," he whispered in my ear and ran his teeth on the edge where I was most ticklish.

A fission of passion shot down my spine.

Ellie pulled the door shut during our little display. Her head was not bowed, but she looked away, giving us space or herself a distraction. Nor did she look behind as Firenze got behind the wheel to drive her to the local ferry. From there her destination options spread from Genoa to Napoli. I hadn't pre-planned which transport she'd board. And Firenze was there to provide assurance that she hadn't been followed and wasn't being watched.

He'd know which one she picked, obviously, and tell Mario, who'd tell me. But other than that, he was forbidden from disclosing his knowledge on orders that came directly from Don Manca himself.

Speaking of the devil.

Mario's grandfather slipped between us to peer at the dust settling. "She's gone?"

"Sì, Aiaiu." Mario's voice was quiet.

"Good. I have work for that one. Hopefully he finds his brain again." He directed an order at Ringo. *"Come. There's a power vacuum forming. We plan."* Poor Ringo, he hadn't stopped staring at the empty road.

He'd fallen hard for my sister and was still denying it.

Worse, I knew Ellie felt the same way. That was why she was running so far and fast from the tranquil security of the island. Even though Leandro was dead, and Dianora was behind bars awaiting trial for shooting her father, I still worried. I'd always worry about my little sister.

Mario tugged me inside. "Sit by my side. You may not understand all the words, but I want your help to hone the arrangements.

As if taking over a seat of family power were a mere holiday to plan.

Ringo brushed by, his mind elsewhere.

Mario shot a hand out and tapped his waistline. "Pay attention."

His friend stared down at the place he'd touched. It matched the almost-healed wound on my husband's side.

"Or what? You'll kill me?"

"It can be arranged," Mario said.

Ringo studied me for a moment. "I bet your wife would jump for a chance to plan it."

I blinked. "I'm not that bloodthirsty…yet." But if he messed with my sister's heart any harder, Mario wouldn't be the one ordering the hit. I would. As it was, Ringo still held a place on my trust but verify list. His methods were suspect to say the least.

Mario smiled and pulled me close. He spoke a sweet nothing aloud that translated poorly, but compared me to one of Ulysses' sea sirens. I frowned at him.

"They lured men to their deaths. I'm not sure that's a compliment."

Don Manca and the others laughed. Then the family patriarch pointed out something I'd missed.

"She understood that. Which means she's one of ours now."

Wow. I had a family with a code and their share of skeletons.

I fit right in.

To quote from one of my favorite movies,

The end is only the beginning...

If you're like me, you want more...
[Looks around, puts a finger on her lips...]
Tell you what, go to this super-secret web page to read a
bonus scene. You may be asked to sign up for a newsletter
there. If you do subscribe, you will get two emails a month
with what's coming next, freebie links, and other great
content, but you can unsubscribe at ANY time.
shh...
caliawilde.com/code/
The password is: Mario

To find more Wilde stories, visit:
https://caliawilde.com

~

Thank you for reading!

— ANNOUNCEMENT —

If your tour of this fictional world was less than a 5-star experience, please don't tell my villains. They get sentimental and silly when not taken seriously. And if you don't care what they think, please go online and review honestly. I love 5-star reviews, but I love YOU more!

Did you leave a review? Tell Calia about it here:
theauthor@caliawilde.com

ABOUT THE AUTHOR

Calia Wilde believes the hero isn't always the good guy. She believes some heroes and heroines cannot play by the rules to get their happily ever after.

She is a writer of misfits, anti-heroes, villains, underdogs, fringe elements, and other tropes that will likely get her barred from polite society.

As a feral Gen-Xer, she spent numerous hours roaming the woods in search of elves, fairies, dragons, or anything that would take her away from the dreaded curse of doing dishes. She once fell off a wardrobe, but instead of landing in Narnia, a very emphatic order of *"Don't tell Mom,"* was decreed. In case you are wondering, yes, she did land on her head.

Rainy days and dark nights landed the author in other worlds between written pages or immersing in her favorite space and time travel TV shows. Whether it was exploring the final frontier or simply disappearing down rabbit holes with shapeshifting aliens, the escape was the same, only the moonscape differed.

One time in Sturgis, she was offered twenty bucks to climb a ladder. She declined as there was some fine print regarding the quest that went beyond conquering a fear of heights and some activities which were definitely illegal for someone her age. But it was there... in that magical realm of bikers, booze, and foul language, that she came into the possession of her very first item of armor... aka, black clothing. The forbidden was in her grasp and became an life-long obsession to avoid anything pastel.

As she searched for a career that would indulge this penchant for wearing black, she stumbled upon the world of special effects and excitedly pursued the art of sleeping in strange hotels, working ungodly hours, and handling anything that could, and would, burn, blind, explode, freeze, or otherwise entertain wildlings like herself.

Her current fictional worlds are forged in a hippie world where music and nature peacefully co-exist away from modern conveniences, like bathtubs. Okay, there's a shower, but she has to share it with spiders. Yuck. Which is why she looks forward to going on the road once more where the hotel may have a real tub. Or a hot tub... maybe a heated pool... please?

So, she BEGS you to leave a review and do a good deed by encouraging others to read her books. With enough fans scattered across the globe, she'll have to travel, right? Then she'll have an excuse to leave the farm.

or

Become an ARC reader and get all the books FIRST.
CaliaWilde.com/become-an-arc-reader/

Walk on the Wilde side here:
CaliaWilde.com

ALSO BY CALIA WILDE

Destroyers Series

Motorcycle Club Romance, Contemporary Action/Adventure Romance Novels and Short Stories

Devils Handmaidens Motorcycle Club

Motorcycle Club Romance, Contemporary Action/Adventure Romance Novels — A shared MC universe with other MC authors

DeSantos Trilogy

Contemporary Romance/Romantic Suspense

Bones Series

Paranormal and Fantasy Romantic Short Stories, Mythology-inspired Romantic Tales

TKI Logistics

Contemporary Romance, Military Romance Short Stories

The Sinister Legacy Duet

Contemporary Mafia Romance Novels

Visit CaliaWilde.com/book-backlist for a full list of current publications.